P9-CDZ-322

Christmas Treats

Patricia Thayer, queen of the rugged rancher, and sparkling new talent Donna Alward bring you...

Montana, Mistletoe, Marriage

Two stories wrapped in one volume!

Praise for Patricia Thayer

Praise for Donna Alward

And look out for Christmas surprises this month in Harlequin Romance!

PATRICIA THAYER
DONNA ALWARD

Montana, Mistletoe, Marriage

Christmas Treats

HARLEQUIN®

TORONTO • NEW YORK • LONDON
AMSTERDAM • PARIS • SYDNEY • HAMBURG
STOCKHOLM • ATHENS • TOKYO • MILAN • MADRID
PRAGUE • WARSAW • BUDAPEST • AUCKLAND

AS-J EW CD

ISBN-13: 978-0-373-17619-9

MONTANA, MISTLETOE, MARRIAGE

First North American Publication 2009.

Copyright © 2009 by Harlequin S.A.

The publisher acknowledges the copyright holders of the individual works as follows:

SNOWBOUND COWBOY
Copyright © 2009 by Patricia Wright

A BRIDE FOR ROCKING H RANCH
Copyright © 2009 by Donna Alward

Recycling programs
for this product may
not exist in your area.

www.eHarlequin.com

Printed in U.S.A.

Patricia Thayer welcomes you to Rocking H Ranch...

Christmas has always been my favorite time of year. I grew up in the Midwest, and as a child one of my first wishes for the holidays was to have snow. Another was for a giant tree that smelled of evergreen and reached all the way to the ceiling in our big old house.

I have a large family—four sisters and three brothers—and though my parents never had a lot, they managed to fill up the bottom of the tree with gifts from Santa. It was years until I realized how truly blessed I was because I had family around to share it with.

As I got older my hopes and dreams changed. Now that I have grandkids, I've discovered that the best presents aren't always wrapped up with a pretty bow. The best are part of everyday life. Like seeing my grandsons' smiles as they run through the waves at the beach, or point up at the moon in wonder. How they grip your hand with complete confidence that you'll keep them safe. How our oldest grandson, who has autism, smiles so brightly when you read his favorite story or sing his favorite song. And how every word he speaks is like a precious gift. No, you can't buy that in any store.

This is my first Christmas story, and I was lucky enough to share it with talented writer Donna Alward. Together we came up with a ranch in Montana, the Rocking H, and two sisters, Kelley and Amelia Hughes.

In my story I created characters who needed to find some holiday joy. When this idea came to me, I kept seeing a five-year-old boy making a Christmas wish. All Jesse Hughes wants is a dad. He even writes it down on a list, and every day he believes that his dad will arrive by Christmas morning. It takes a Montana snow blizzard and my hero and heroine getting stranded together just two weeks before Christmas.

Amelia, a single mother, is afraid to trust another man again. Boone Gifford carries a burden with him that makes him think he doesn't deserve a family. Somehow these two began to believe in a Montana Christmas miracle and never had to unwrap one gift.

In Donna's story, Kelley enlists the help of chef Mack Dennison to help her create the perfect Hughes family Christmas. Somehow they both start to realize that the most perfect gift could very well be each other…if they're willing to open their hearts.

My hope for all of you is to receive the kind of gift that isn't always found under the tree. Just look around and count your blessings.

Happy Holidays

Patricia Thayer

CHAPTER ONE

SHE'D DONE IT NOW.

Amelia Hughes stared out the windshield at the blowing snow and thought about her rash decision to drive into town in spite of blizzard warnings. She had thought she could outrun the storm. In her haste to get back to the ranch, she had hit a slick spot, and the truck had slid off the snow-packed road onto the soft shoulder.

"Mom, we got stuck!"

"We don't know that for sure," she said, wondering what her penance should be for lying to a five-year-old boy. In an attempt to right her wrong, she eased her foot onto the gas peddle causing the tires to spin and the back of the truck to slide further off the road.

Great. With a sigh, Amelia stopped her attempt to regain traction, and turned to meet her child's wide brown-eyed gaze. His stocking cap covered a head full of whiskey-colored curls, and light freckles dusted his small nose and rosy cheeks. Jesse Thomas Hughes was her everything.

Somehow she had to get them out of this. After all, she'd lived in rural western Montana all her life. She came from sturdy, frontier stock. Her great-grandparents mined this land, finally turning to ranching. They never gave up, nor would she.

She gripped the wheel and went back to work. Yet, no matter what direction she turned the wheel, or how gently she worked the gas peddle, she couldn't get the old truck to move forward. She finally stopped to save fuel. They might need heat if they had to spend the night here. No, she refused to think about that. They had hours of daylight left.

"Boy, Aunt Kelley is going to be mad."

"No, Aunt Kelley won't be mad." Another lie just rolled off her tongue. "But maybe we shouldn't tell her. She has a lot to worry about with taking Grandma Ruby to the hospital."

Jesse nodded. "Okay. Maybe if we wish really hard someone will come by and save us."

Amelia wasn't so sure that was going to work, either. There wasn't much reason for anyone to be on this road. Everyone else was at home heeding the storm warning. She'd only gone out to buy supplies before they'd gotten snowbound.

Normally the Hughes household was prepared for bad weather, but the December storm caught them off guard. With Gram's illness, everyone had been distracted getting her into Helena and the hospital.

Jesse turned to her again. "Maybe we should call Aunt Kelley. She'll know what to do."

Amelia didn't doubt it. Her older sister pretty much ran the cattle operation, while Amelia handled the household. It wasn't that she didn't love taking care of the family, but she'd also like her sister to listen to some of her ideas for the ranch. Kelley hadn't even trusted her to handle things while she was in Helena, and made arrangements to hire a ranch hand to help out.

The last thing Amelia wanted was for her sister to know she'd already messed up things in her absence. But what was more important, she needed to get herself and her son out of this weather.

She pulled out her cell phone. "I've got a better idea. I'll call the sheriff."

Boone Gifford was a Texas boy, born and bred.

He had never been crazy about cold weather or snow. Now he was in the middle of a blizzard outside of Rebel Ridge, Montana. He'd only come here because he'd given his word. And Boone never went back on his word. So the sooner he got to the Rocking H, the sooner he could leave for a warmer climate.

He swiped his gloved hand over the windshield to clear away the condensation. It didn't help. Visibility was nil. Even reducing his speed to a crawl hadn't helped much. He wasn't even sure where he was.

Absently he rubbed his sore shoulder, reminding him of his last job on the off-shore oil rig and the accident that nearly took his life. He'd survived, but he would never forget the men who'd died that day. Especially one.

He shook away the memory to concentrate on his task. Not an easy one, either. The wind gusted again, continuing to make it difficult to keep his vehicle on the road. His grip tightened around the steering wheel. If he had a brain, he'd never have attempted to get to the Hughes ranch today.

No, he needed to finish this, once and for all. He needed to see Amelia Hughes, then he could move on with a clear conscience.

Boone kept his gaze sharp as his new four-wheel-drive truck crept along the dangerous terrain. Lucky for him, his tires could handle mud and snow. Suddenly he saw flashing emergency lights up ahead. As he got closer, he realized it was a truck parked at a funny angle along the shoulder.

So he wasn't the only crazy person out here. He stopped in the middle of the road, then, pulling the collar up on his coat, he climbed out. Fighting the sharp wind, he made his way to the embankment and the truck cab.

"Hey, is there anyone in there?" he called, and banged on the window.

He blinked the snow from his eyes as the window came down and a woman's face appeared. "Oh, thank God you came by. My son and I went off the road and we're stuck. If you could just help us to our ranch? It's just up the road a few miles."

"The Rocking H?" Boone asked.

"Yes." The pretty woman smiled, lighting up her rich green eyes. "Oh, you must be the hand from the Sky High Ranch. I'm Amelia Hughes."

So he'd found her. As Russ had described, she was a pretty brunette. Not wanting to stand here and give her an explanation, he gave her a quick nod. "Boone Gifford. Look, we need to get out of this, and my truck seems to be our best bet." He pulled open the door and helped the woman out of the truck, then behind her he saw the small boy.

"My son, Jesse," Amelia called, fighting the wind.

The boy slid across the seat. His eyes were wide along with his smile. A sudden tightness gripped Boone's chest.

"Hey, kid."

"Hi." The boy cocked his head to the side and grinned. "Are you my Christmas wish?"

The normal ten-minute trip had taken nearly thirty by the time Boone pulled the truck up to the back door. Amelia finally released a breath. She climbed out of the truck and carrying two grocery bags, trudged her way to the porch. Boone Gifford swung Jesse up into his arms and followed her.

"We made it," Amelia cried as she stepped into the big kitchen. She set down her groceries on the long table. She wanted to drop to the floor and kiss it. She didn't want to think about what could have happened if they had been left out there.

"Yeah, we made it," Jesse mimicked as he came into the room.

Boone put her son down, but Jesse wasn't leaving his side. Amelia noticed the child's budding hero worship.

She pulled off her hat and shook out her long hair. "How about some coffee, Mr. Gifford?"

"Please, call me Boone." He took off his cowboy hat and unwrapped the scarf from his neck. "Yes, please, I wouldn't mind a cup to warm up."

"Can I have some hot chocolate, Mom?"

Amelia took her son's coat and hung it on a hook beside the mud room door. "Yes, you can, but I want you to go change out of your jeans into some warm sweats."

He tugged off his cap, revealing his curly dark hair. "Ah, Mom. I want to talk to Boone some more."

That was the problem. She had to nix this before her son drove the ranch hand crazy. "You can when you get back, but right now there's a storm coming and we need to take care of the livestock, too."

"'Kay," he murmured and walked out of the room.

"I apologize for all my son's questions on the way home."

"Not a problem. He seems like a good kid."

"I think so, but I'm a little biased." She smiled and he smiled back before he turned away to the window.

Boone Gifford wasn't what you'd call classically handsome, but you took notice of the man. His ebony eyes were deep set, his jaw was chiseled with a shadow of a beard. His thick hair was coal black with a slight wave and long enough to brush the back of his collar. He was tall, well-over six feet, with shoulders so broad it made the room seem crowded.

Boone turned back toward her, catching her looking at him.

"Looks like this storm is going to be a rough one," he said, his gaze holding hers. "I should get out to the barn while I have a chance."

She cleared her throat, but couldn't remember what she wanted to say. She nodded, then went to the counter and began making coffee. "Good idea."

"Okay, you have anything special you need done?"

"My sister, Kelley, left written instructions in the tack room. And your sleeping quarters are right next door."

He nodded. "I'll go check out things and be back shortly." He started for the door, then stopped. "What did your son mean when he asked if I was his Christmas wish?"

She froze. "Oh, you know how kids are. It's only two weeks before Christmas and he has his list of what he wants. I'm sorry if he bothered you."

"It's not a problem." He paused again. "What exactly is he asking for?"

Jesse walked into the room. "I want a Dad."

Boone hurried into the barn and forced the door shut against the bitter cold wind. He was a coward. He'd had the perfect chance to tell her the real reason he was here. Instead he let her continue to think he was the ranch hand who'd been hired to help out. Why not? Amelia Hughes needed help, and he could at least hang around until the other guy showed up.

Boone walked down the center aisle to find everything neat and orderly. There were nearly a dozen stalls lining the walls, four with horses. He found he was a little envious.

Back in Texas his barn had looked a lot like this one. He'd taken pride in all the work he and his dad had put into the Last Dollar Ranch. The house had been far from a showplace, because they put every penny into the care of the stock. Then, after the bank took over, the ranch fell into total neglect. But not for long. Thanks to the financial settlement from the accident, he had the money and the opportunity to get it back.

Just as soon as he paid his other debt.

Suddenly a big chocolate Labrador appeared and began barking. "Hey, fella. Where'd you come from?" Boone held out his hand and the animal approached, then began wagging his tail. Once the dog relaxed, Boone petted him. He noticed the animal's full flanks. He grinned after further examination. "So you're a gal and a mother-to-be. And by the looks of it, you don't have long to go."

The dog barked in agreement.

Boone stood. "Come on, show me around?"

They headed toward the immaculate tack room and the dog's bed lined with blankets. He also found the list of boldly printed instructions. The next room was the sleeping quarters for the hired hand. A single bunk and a dresser, plus a wall heater. This wasn't meant for him. And before the real ranch hand showed up, he'd best tell Amelia the truth.

His thoughts turned to the pretty woman with the rich green eyes. She had a full, tempting mouth that caused his body to tighten, making him realize how alone he'd been the past six months.

He shook off the wayward thoughts. What would Amelia Hughes do when she realized he hadn't been exactly truthful? He rubbed the back of his neck. Maybe he should just hand over the envelope addressed to her and head out.

The wind howled outside. He wasn't going anywhere right now, and maybe not for a while.

And there was Jesse. He needed to know about his daddy, especially since Russ Eldon had died before he got the chance to come and meet his son.

Now all Boone had to do was tell a little boy he would never get his Christmas wish.

CHAPTER TWO

AMELIA PACED THE KITCHEN, occasionally glancing out the window at the blowing snow. She couldn't see a thing. And according to the forecast, the weather wasn't going to improve for at least three or four days. How bad was it going to get? She looked toward the barn, barely able to see the red structure. Suddenly, she was happy Boone Gifford had showed up.

The phone rang and she picked it up on the second ring. "Hello."

"Amelia. It's Kelley."

"Kelley, hi. Is Gram okay?"

"Yes. I got her settled in her room and she's resting right now."

"That's good." Amelia knew how hard it had been to convince seventy-five-year-old Ruby Hughes to have this procedure done.

"Well, the doctor had to sedate her so she'd be relaxed." There was a pause. "How are you and Jesse doing? I'm worried about this storm, Amelia. It's going to get bad."

Amelia glanced outside again. The wind was blowing heavy snow. "We'll be fine, Kel."

"But what if you can't get out?"

"I have help."

"Oh, good. So Joe sent over the hand from Sky High Ranch."

She wasn't going to tell her sister that he had already rescued her and Jesse. "Yes, he's moving his things into the barn and checking on the horses."

"I'm glad you're not there alone."

So was she, but she'd never tell Kelley. "I know you don't think so, but I can handle things. I've lived out here as long as you have."

"I know, but I can't help being worried."

"Don't, because then Gram will worry, too. She's got to be your only concern right now. Mine is the ranch and Jesse." She went to the high counter that divided the kitchen from the dining room and glanced further into the great room to find her son sitting in front of the television watching a video.

Kelley still wasn't convinced and rattled off a list of instructions. Amelia heard the back door shut and turned as Boone walked into the kitchen. His dark eyes met hers, and her throat suddenly went dry.

"Amelia...Amelia. Are you there?"

She shook away her wandering thoughts and turned back. "Yes, I'm here. Look, Kel, Jesse needs me so I better go. Call after the surgery tomorrow. Bye."

Amelia hung up the phone before her sister gave her more things to do.

"I came for that coffee." He removed his hat and coat revealing a dark-green flannel shirt.

"Sure." Amelia swung away from the distraction and went to the freshly brewed pot and grabbed two mugs. After filling it, she placed them on the table. "Cream or sugar?"

He shook his head. "No, black's fine, ma'am." The large brown dog lumbered into the room.

"Oh, Izzy. I forgot all about you." She glanced at Boone. "Thanks for bringing her to the house. She's pretty close to her delivery time."

Amelia went over and petted the dog. The animal basked in the attention, then wandered over to the warm kitchen hearth and lay down on the rug.

"Have a seat," she offered, and sat down across from him. "That was my sister, Kelley, on the phone. She wanted to make sure you got here." Amelia took a sip of coffee. "She was checking up on me, too. To see if I was staying out of trouble."

"She's probably worried."

Amelia nodded. Kelley had watched over her since they

were little; since their dad died and their mother left them here for Grandma Ruby to raise. "She'd have a fit if she knew I'd gone out in the storm." She met his dark gaze. "I can't thank you enough for showing up when you did."

Boone knew he should tell her his real reason for being on the road today. But then he saw Amelia's nervousness. "You already have. Besides, you and Jesse are safe now." He set down his mug. "I checked the supply of wood on the porch. There seems to be plenty for a few days. I'll go out before dark and move more from the side of the house."

"That's a good idea since the radio says it's only getting worse. The roads are impassable. Not uncommon for this part of the country."

"Did they say how long the weather system will last?"

"Through Thursday, at least."

Great. He couldn't leave for three days. He took a long drink of coffee. This was a bad idea all around. "I should get settled in." He stood and carried his cup to the sink when Jesse rushed into the kitchen.

The boy smiled. "Oh, Boone, you're back."

"Not for long."

The child frowned. "You can't leave now. Mom's going to fix lunch." The boy turned to his mother. "Mom, will you make egg salad?"

"I can."

"It's the best," the boy bragged. "Everybody says so. I even like it, but not as much as peanut butter and jelly. That's because Mom makes the bread and her special jelly. It's peach. That's my favorite. What's your favorite, Boone?" The kid finally took a breath.

"I'd say peach is probably at the top of my list, too."

The boy grinned. "I bet Mom would fix you peanut butter and jelly if you want."

"Jesse," his mother called, "slow down. We can have both for lunch." Amelia glanced up at the clock over the sink. "Why don't you go and wash your hands?"

Jesse started to argue, but at a look from his mother turned and hurried down the hall.

"I apologize for my son. Outside of seasonal ranch hands, he's doesn't have many men around."

Boone had learned as much from the friendly waitress in town at the diner. The Hughes women were well respected and admired around here. "From what I can see, you've done a fine job with him and this place."

She glanced away. "Tnank you. My family helps a lot."

He nodded in agreement. "Family is a good thing."

"Do you have family? A wife…children?"

"No," he said, trying not to react. He'd lost any part of that dream two years ago.

She sighed and refilled their coffee mugs. "Since you'll be around for a few days, there's something you should know." She paused. "When Jesse started kindergarten this year, he realized his classmates have dads. Everyone except him. So he came up with this crazy idea that all he had to do was ask for one. So on the top of his Christmas list he has the word *Dad*."

Boone nodded. Great. And here he'd arrived with news that would make it impossible for the boy to get that wish. "And his father?"

She shook her head. "His father has never been involved in Jesse's life, nor at this stage do I want him to be."

Boone couldn't blame her for that. "I guess every boy wants a dad."

"But he can't go around picking one out, either. I'll have a talk with him."

This was getting complicated. "Maybe I should leave now." He stood. "I mean, go to the barn."

"No, you're not going to stay out in a cold barn all day. I'll handle Jesse. I just wanted you to know the situation."

Amelia got up, walked to the refrigerator and took out the ingredients for the salad. When she bent over he caught the appealing shape of her bottom and long legs. His attention was drawn upward as she went to the counter, took a loaf of bread out from under a towel and began slicing it.

"Is there anything I can do?" he asked, knowing he couldn't just sit there and ogle this woman.

"You can get the plates down from the cupboard." She nodded overhead.

Boone walked up behind her. Reaching over her head, he caught a whiff of her shampoo. Something lemony. Something that normally wouldn't be sexy to him. It was now. He gripped the plates and carried them to the table before he got himself into trouble.

Jesse came in. "I'll help you, Boone."

The boy pulled flatware from the drawer and placed it beside the plates.

"Good job," Boone said.

"Gram Ruby says I'm her best helper," Jesse said proudly. "I help Kelley with the horses, too." Those big brown eyes widened. "I can help you, too."

"Jesse Thomas," his mother called. "Don't even think about leaving the house in this storm."

"Ah, Mom. If I get lost, Izzy can find me."

At the mention of her name the dog looked up. "Izzy isn't in any shape to go traipsing around in this weather," Amelia said.

"What if Boone gets lost? Who will find him?"

Amelia swung around to look at Boone. She was asking for help.

"I strung a rope from the barn to here. And believe me, once I get back there I'm staying put."

The wind howled outside, and suddenly the lights flickered, then finally died.

"Oh, no," Amelia said. Although it was afternoon, the room was dim, only illuminated by the fire from the hearth.

"Do you have a generator?" Boone asked.

"Yes, it's in the mud room." She led him out to the enclosed porch and to a closet.

Boone examined the old machinery. "Have you used it recently?"

"Not since last spring. And only for a few hours. Gram had it checked out just last month."

Jesse poked his head in. "And the man said she needed to get a new one," he volunteered. "Gram was looking in the catalog. She showed me a picture of the one she wants." He looked up at both adults. "You want to see it?"

"Not now, honey." She turned to Boone. "Do you think you can start it?"

He threw a switch, then pulled the cord to get the motor running. He stood back. "I'm just not sure how reliable it is. It's best to keep both fireplaces going. You can sleep in front of the living room one tonight."

"Oh, boy. Can you sleep there, too, Boone? Can he, Mom, huh?"

Boone watched the pretty brunette blush. "I don't think Mr. Gifford would be happy to share space with a rambunctious five-year-old."

The boy wrinkled his nose. "That means I jump around too much. But I'll promise to be quiet."

"I appreciate the offer, son, but maybe you and your mother should have the sofa space. I'll make sure you have plenty of firewood to keep you both warm." He started to walk off.

"Wait, Boone," Amelia called as he started out. "I have to agree with my son. You can't sleep in the barn, not without electricity. You'll move in here."

CHAPTER THREE

BOONE WASN'T SURE how to react to Amelia's statement. True, he couldn't sleep in the barn, but invading their personal space was a different story. He hadn't signed up for this.

"Maybe the electricity will be back on by then."

Amelia frowned. "I take it you haven't lived in Montana long. This outage could last days."

"I'm originally from West Texas. We don't get many blizzards."

"Well, we do. So unless you want to freeze, you better decide to camp out with us tonight. You can have the small room off the kitchen." She led them back inside and pointed to the eight-paneled door across the room. "One of its walls is the back of the fireplace. It stays pretty warm in there."

He hated doing this. "I don't mean to put you out, ma'am." He had no business being here in the first place.

"You'll only put me out if I have to worry about you sleeping in that cold barn."

He felt a strange feeling in the center of his gut. It'd been a while since a woman had been concerned about him. "I would have been okay. The animals are my responsibility."

"Their stalls are pretty well insulated. And there's another generator out there, but we don't usually use it unless it's absolutely necessary."

He was surprised how well Amelia Hughes handled the emergency. If she was nervous about the situation, she didn't show it.

"Seems you have everything under control," he told her.

"I'm fine as long as we stay in the house and have enough food. And we do. Since the stove is propane, I'll be able to cook."

Boone stood at the counter, the only thing that separated the kitchen from the dining area, then past it was the living room with two overstuffed sofas angled toward a huge stone fireplace.

He looked up to see the exposed beams, then down at the polished hardwood floors. No doubt the place had probably been remodeled over the years. He found he liked the mixture of both the old and the new.

His attention was drawn back to the woman wandering around turning off unneeded lights. She smiled and he felt a funny tightness in his chest. Her green-eyed gaze locked with his, then quickly she turned away.

"How about I finish making us lunch?"

Boone nodded. "I could eat."

"So could I," Jesse chimed in. "I'm real hungry."

She messed up her son's hair. "You're always hungry."

The boy grinned. "That's cause I'm growing."

The twosome walked into the kitchen, and Boone found he enjoyed listening to the bantering between mother and son.

Something tugged at his heart as his thoughts turned to Russ. His friend would be happy at how well his boy had turned out. Now all Boone had to do was find a way to tell the kid's mother about her son's father.

As Amelia mixed the egg salad, she could feel Boone watching her. It had been a long time since a man had been in the Hughes house. Sad, but true. She hadn't had time, or any desire, to attempt a relationship. Since Russ, she hadn't let anyone get close to her. Not that men had rushed to her door. If one did, Kelley would probably be there to give him the third degree. Her big sister had always been Amelia's protector. She'd also sat with Amelia during the rough times after Jesse's father left. Later she'd coached her through labor and the delivery of her son. And she loved Jesse as much as Amelia did.

What would Kelley think about Boone Gifford? That he was handsome? Her sister didn't get her head turned easily. Not when she worked side by side with ranch hands that drifted from job to job. She couldn't afford to.

Neither could Amelia, but she couldn't deny that she'd taken notice of Boone Gifford. She sighed. She had to keep reminding herself that he was a stranger. Thank goodness Kelley had checked him out.

Amelia handed out the sandwiches and poured the milk.

She sat down and glanced at the smile on her son's face as he chatted with Boone. It was Jesse who'd suffered the most from his father choosing to desert them. With just women around, a boy craved male companionship.

She turned her attention to Boone. He wasn't the kind of man either one of them needed. He wasn't even from Montana, but West Texas, and she had no doubt he would be going back. No way was she getting mixed up again with a guy who was just passing through.

Jesse said something, and Boone managed a smile. Her attention went to his mouth and the tiny lines bracketing it, which only seemed to add to his rugged features.

Suddenly he looked up. She swallowed, feeling the strange tension in her stomach. This was not good.

"Mom!"

"What?" She turned to her son.

"I asked if Boone and me can play cards."

"Honey, Boone isn't here to entertain you."

"It's not a bother," Boone said, then turned to her son. "First, we need to help clean up."

Amelia watched as her son picked up his empty plate and followed Boone to the sink. The big, tall cowboy took up too much space in the kitchen, making her feel crowded and edgy. And a lot more. She stood, too, but kept the needed distance between her and the man. Boone Gifford was a stranger and he would be leaving soon.

She needed to remember that.

The afternoon dragged on as the snow continued to fall. Boone had played card games with Jesse to keep the boy occupied. Amelia kept busy going around the house, closing off rooms to conserve the heat. She'd brought out candles and extra bedding from upstairs. When Boone had offered to help her she put him off. Instead, she began chopping vegetables for supper.

"Jesse. I think it's time to put the cards away."

"Ah, Mom, I'm winning."

"You've been playing for the last hour. I need your help to prepare for tonight."

Boone glanced over. As the afternoon turned toward evening, she seemed to grow nervous. Was it only the threatening storm, or was it him?

"Your mom's right." He got up from the table. "Besides, I need to check the animals." He headed to the coat hook, pulled on his sheepskin-lined jacket and wrapped the scarf around his neck.

"Boone, would you mind bringing up Izzy's food?"

"Sure." He reached down and petted the dog. "You want to go with me, girl?"

The large animal walked to the back door and waited.

Boone tugged his hat low on his head and pulled on his gloves. He went out the back door noticing the snow had slowed but not the wind. He grabbed hold of the anchor rope he'd rigged earlier and began to traipse through the knee-high snow toward the barn.

Inside, he stomped off the clinging snow before he fed and watered the horses, then retrieved the dog's food and headed back.

Izzy finished her business and didn't have any trouble finding her way to the house. Boone set the food in the mud room, then went to his truck and got his duffel bag.

Back on the porch, he found a bundled-up Jesse waiting.

"Mom said I can help you carry in some wood."

"Good. I can use a strong helper." He glanced toward the window, not surprised to see Amelia. He nodded to her and went to load up the boy's small arms with split logs. Once inside, they stacked it neatly beside the fireplaces. After three trips, he decided they had enough to get through until morning.

Amelia had been working, too. She had a pot of homemade stew simmering on the stove, filling the kitchen with a heavenly aroma. He carried his duffel bag into the small room off the kitchen where he found the double bed already made up with snowy white sheets and two heavy blankets.

Amelia appeared at the doorway. "My grandfather stayed in here during his long illness. Gram Ruby never changed the room back to her sewing room."

"I won't disturb anything," Boone told her as he set his bag on the cedar chest at the end of the bed.

"It's okay," Jesse said as he walked in. "'Cause when I'm sick I get to stay here. I even threw up all over the blankets." He made a face. "It was gross, but Mom didn't even get mad."

Boone hid a smile. "That's good to know."

"Jesse, why don't we let Boone get settled in?" She motioned for her son to come with her.

The boy obeyed, but paused at the doorway. "Can we still play cards later?"

"If it's okay with your mom."

The boy swung around to Amelia, looking for the okay.

"We'll see, Jesse. Come on, you can help me with the bread." She looked at Boone. "Supper will be ready about six, unless you get hungry before that."

"I'll be there at six." He looked at Jesse. "Why don't you come and get me, so I don't miss your mama's stew?"

When the boy smiled he could see a strong resemblance to Russ, but the physical likeness was where it ended. Did he have a right to burst in here and intrude on their lives? Yes, the boy needed to know that his father had cared about him and wanted to come and meet him. He had to at least tell the kid's mother, then she could decide what to do. What would Boone's announcement do to Amelia Hughes?

Amelia tugged her son's arm. "We'll see you at supper." She stepped back, leaving the door open to help circulate the sparse heat.

Boone sat down on the bed and lit the candle on the nightstand. The daylight was quickly fading. He pulled off his boots, rubbing one foot over the other. Once he'd stimulated warmth back into his toes, he lay down and rested his head against the feather pillow.

He couldn't help but think back to six months ago. It had never been his dream to work as a roustabout on an oil rig off the coast of Galveston, Texas. And that was where he'd met Russell Eldon.

Boone hadn't cared much about making friends, only about making money to buy back the ranch he'd lost. Russ wanted to give something to the child he'd abandoned, and he couldn't stop talking about it.

Sharing close quarters, Boone had listened to Russ's story. How at twenty-one he'd gotten a girl pregnant. In a panic, he'd taken off, even before he knew if she had the baby or not.

About a year ago, Russ had learned that he had a son. For the past months he'd worked on the oil rig to make fast money so he could help with support before he came to meet his child. Jesse Hughes.

It wasn't to be. Last summer they'd been evacuated when a hurricane headed for the platform, but the last helicopter crashed and they all ended up in the gulf.

A shiver went through Boone as he recalled that awful night. The rough waters that kept pulling him under. The excruciating pain in his injured shoulder. His struggle to stay conscious. Through it all, he kept hearing Russ's voice, telling him not to give up. The guy had been there with him, keeping him afloat until help came.

Boone shut his eyes, seeing Russ's face as the rough waters took him down, all the time knowing it should have been him who died that night.

If Russ hadn't had to rescue him, Jesse wouldn't be without a father.

CHAPTER FOUR

THROUGH THE FOG Boone heard a feminine voice whisper his name. A rush of sensations drifted through him, and his body stirred with longing. He groaned, wanting the dream to go on. Then came the gentlest of touches, and warmth shot through him.

She spoke his name again and he blinked, aching to see her, praying reality would be even better. When he opened his eyes, he saw Amelia Hughes's face in the dim candlelight.

She smiled shyly. "Hi."

"Hi," he returned.

Her gaze was guarded and she stepped back from the bedside. "Sorry to wake you, but you said you wanted us to let you know when it's suppertime. Jesse wasn't sure what to do when he found you asleep."

He wiped a hand across his eyes, taking time to ease his racing pulse. "Thanks, I'm glad you woke me." He swung his legs off the bed and sat up. "I don't usually fall asleep on the job." He checked his watch to see that two hours had truly passed.

"It's probably the boredom," she said. "There isn't much to do trapped in the house."

He definitely hadn't been bored since coming here. The brisk chill in the room made him realize he wasn't going anywhere, not for a while, anyway. He noticed Amelia wore a long sweater that covered her all the way down past her shapely hips. On her feet were heavy, wool socks.

"How's the wood holding out?"

"I've been keeping both fireplaces going, but even after closing off the upstairs, it's still chilly. We're managing for now, but tonight the temperature is predicted to drop well below freezing."

Boone pulled on his boots, trying not to think about the intimacy of her watching him. He stood and walked toward her. At six foot three, he towered over most women, but Amelia was also tall. He liked that. She tilted her head back slightly as her emerald eyes met his gaze. Suddenly his mouth went dry. There wasn't much about this woman that he didn't like. She was definitely trouble.

"I'll bring in more wood."

"It can wait until later," she said. "I don't want your supper to get cold."

He wasn't used to anyone worrying about him. "Okay." With a nod he followed her into the warmer kitchen. The table was adorned with candles and three place settings.

"Hi, Boone." Jesse came over and took his hand, leading him to the seat at the table. "Mom made stew for supper. It's my favorite."

Amelia placed her hands on her hips. "Hey, I thought you liked my macaroni and cheese best."

The boy nodded his head. "I like that, too. I like everything you make." He turned to Boone. "Mom's the best cook. She makes pies for the diner in town. Everybody loves them."

"Jesse," she warned. "Stop bragging."

"I'm only saying what's true, Mom. Even Mrs. Hoffman at church said so. She told my teacher, Miss Claire, that Mom's a good catch."

Amelia gasped. "Jesse Thomas Hughes you're not supposed to listen to other people's conversations."

"But I didn't, Mom. They were talking right to me."

Boone tried hard not to smile as a blushing Amelia came to the table. She avoided his gaze as she placed the soup tureen in the center, then went back for the basket of rolls.

She sat across from Boone. "Enjoy this meal, because if this storm keeps up, no one will be eating anything but canned soup."

"Are we going to be snowed in for Christmas?" The boy looked worried. "And what about Izzy's puppies?"

Amelia spooned up a bowl of stew for Boone. "She's not on her own, we're here to help if she needs us."

Boone took the warm bowl. "Thank you." He looked at Jesse. "I think she can handle it."

"Have you ever seen puppies born?" Jesse asked Boone.

"No, but I've helped with calves and foals. Believe me, mamas know what to do."

Jesse gave his mother a curious look. "Mom, did you know what to do when I was born?"

Even in the dim light, Boone watched another blush cover Amelia's face. "Well, not everything, but I had Aunt Kelley and Gram Ruby with me. And the doctor, of course."

Still looking bewildered, the boy picked up his spoon. "Do I get to help Izzy, too?"

Amelia placed a napkin on her lap. "Well, I'm not sure."

"It depends on Izzy," Boone jumped in. "She might just want to do it all by herself."

"Is that why Mom put a big box in the closet?"

Boone nodded. "So Izzy can have some privacy."

Before Jesse could ask another question, Amelia spoke up. "Let's say grace so we can eat."

Jesse took his mother's hand, then held out the other to Boone. It had been a long time since he had much to pray about, but maybe it was time he started. He took the boy's hand, then reached across the table for Amelia's. For a second he allowed himself to think about a home and family.

Amelia liked the feel of Boone's large hand. Too much. The man was little more than a stranger. That alone sent up warning signals. She definitely couldn't let herself romanticize the situation. She let that happen once, not again. She had a lot more at stake this time than to be foolish enough to allow some good-looking cowboy turn her head.

She glanced at her son as he talked with Boone. It didn't take much to get a five-year-old's attention. Especially since all he'd ever wanted was a father.

"Are you going to be here for Christmas, Boone?"

"Not sure, son. I'm hoping to be back in Texas by then."

"What about your job?" Amelia asked.

His gaze shifted to her as he raised his spoon. "It's temporary. I'd always planned to head back home someday."

"Texas," Jesse said. "Do you have kids there?"

Boone shook his head. "No family to speak of. Not anymore."

The boy's eyes rounded. "Then why not stay here? You can work for Mom and Aunt Kelley."

"Jesse," she said in her best warning tone. Her son had to stop this. "You know we only hire hands during calving season."

"But, Mom…"

Boone stepped in. "It's a nice offer, son, but I'm going to buy my own ranch, in Texas."

"Oh…" Jesse didn't hide his disappointment.

Amelia felt a twinge of the same. She glanced at Boone to find him watching her. Her breathing grew heavy as she locked on his mesmerizing gaze. This was crazy. She'd only just met the man and suddenly she was wanting him to stay around.

Boone turned back to her son. "You see, Jesse, I've been wanting one particular place for a long time, and now I have a chance to buy it."

The boy looked thoughtful. "Hey, you could buy a ranch in Montana." He turned to his mother. "Right, Mom?"

Hours later the house was quiet as Boone stretched out on the double bed, staring out into the darkness, trying to sleep. But the words that Amelia Hughes spoke earlier were still swimming around in his head:

Boone's place is in Texas, and ours is here in Montana.

He knew it shouldn't bother him, but it had. He'd never had much as a kid.

Years ago, Hank and Jolene Gifford hadn't been much more than day laborers until they scraped enough money together to buy some land of their own. With their old truck loaded up, their son and all their worldly belongings, they arrived in West Texas and their first home.

Many nights, he'd slept in the bed of the pickup until the house was built. His mother took a job in town to help them survive as his father ran a small herd. Boone had worked hard as a boy and continued as a man, building the family ranch.

Their hard work finally paid off until the day he lost both his parents in an accident. He couldn't run the place without his dad.

Now at the age of thirty, he was getting a second chance. Nothing was going to keep him from his dreams this time.

He stood, went to his duffel bag and found the manila envelope tucked under a pair of his jeans. He knew what was inside without even looking. All Russ Eldon's personal effects. Everything his friend had wanted to give his son.

Boone sighed. Coming here wasn't supposed to be so complicated. He'd planned to hand over everything to Amelia Hughes and just leave. Instead he was trapped here in her home, and he was feeling things for the woman he had no business feeling.

He needed to get out of here and fast.

That same husky soft voice called his name again. Boone looked toward the doorway and saw Amelia. Holding a hurricane lantern, she stood shadowed in the dim light. Her dark hair was slightly mussed and she had a blanket bundled around her trim body. Her gaze was questioning.

Boone drew another breath, trying to fight the urges she invoked in him. He zipped the bag and went to her.

"Is there a problem?" he asked.

"I think we're going to need more firewood."

He suddenly became aware of the chill. "Maybe you should turn on the heat, too."

She released a breath. "I'm just worried that the generator won't hold out."

He nodded. "How's Jesse? Is he warm enough?"

She smiled. "He's fine and sound asleep. How are you doing in here?"

"It's not bad." Hell, it was cold.

She smiled at his lie. "Okay, we turn on the heat. But I'll need to close the vents upstairs."

"I'll help you."

He followed her through the kitchen, checking on Jesse as they went. The boy was layered with blankets on the sofa. He followed Amelia up the steps to the second floor where she opened the door at the top.

Amelia felt the drop in temperature immediately. "Oh, burr, it's freezing."

"Colder than a witch's..." Boone began. "It's darn cold." He stood behind her and held up the lantern. "Go back downstairs, Amelia. I can handle this."

She turned, nearly bumping into him. "But I know where all the registers are."

With a nod from him, she headed into her grandmother's bedroom. They worked quickly to shut off the vents, then moved on to Jesse's room. Next, they went into hers. This had been her childhood bedroom and not much had changed since then. It seemed strange to have Boone here. There hadn't been a man in here ever, not even Jesse's father.

She knelt down next to her twin bed, and worked the iron grate, but it wouldn't budge. "Stubborn thing."

Boone appeared, shinning more light. "Here, let me try."

Before she could get out of the way, he leaned over her, and his hard chest brushed against her back. She felt his muscles strain as he fought the stubborn lever and won.

He didn't move away, and strangely, Amelia didn't want him to.

"Where to next?" His voice vibrated against her ear. "Your sister's room?"

"Kelley doesn't live in the house anymore. A few years ago she moved into the foreman's cottage." She stopped her rambling and took a breath to relax. It didn't help. Was she so starved for a man that the slightest contact set her off?

With this man, yes.

He finally moved back. "Then I guess we're finished," he said. "We should head downstairs."

Still on her knees, she turned to face him. In the dim shadows, they were close in the confined space. Dangerously close.

Suddenly she heard her name called. "Mom! Mom! Where are you?"

She broke eye contact, got to her feet and hurried into the hallway. "I'm coming, Jesse."

"Hurry, Mom. Izzy's having her puppies."

CHAPTER FIVE

BOONE FOLLOWED AMELIA downstairs to find the mother-to-be in her box in the pantry. Seeing her owner, Izzy whimpered.

"See, Mom?"

Amelia knelt down inside the narrow enclosure next to her son and gently stroked the dog's head. "What's the matter, girl? Are your babies getting impatient to be born?"

In answer, the animal licked her hand and panted heavily.

"Mom, is Izzy having her puppies now?"

Amelia stood and backed out of the small space. "It looks like it, honey. Maybe we should give her some privacy."

The boy didn't like the idea. "But what if she needs us?"

"She might. So we need to get some towels and thread to tie off the puppies' cords in case she needs help."

When the boy started to argue, Boone spoke up, "Come on, Jesse, I'll help you, too. Do you know where the thread is?"

With the boy's nod, the threesome gathered the things needed and returned for the expected delivery. Wrapped in a blanket, with the lantern next to him, Jesse sat in the doorway waiting.

Boone stood holding another light overhead, and watched in awe as Amelia coaxed the Labrador to push out the first tiny puppy. Jesse gasped in delight, and showed even more excitement as the second and third came along.

"You're doing fine, girl," Amelia spoke to her patient as she wiped off each new arrival. "Here comes another," she said, then amended that. "Oh, and another."

Boone handed Jesse the light and instructed him how to hold it. Then he jumped in and assisted Amelia so none of the puppies would be lost.

By the end, the litter count added up to eight healthy puppies. Amelia gently helped clean the last arrival, and gave it to the mother to begin nursing. Then she worked quickly to removed the soiled towels and replace them with fresh bedding.

Boone took the dirty towels and set them aside, then helped Jesse bring some food and water for the new mother.

"Mom, can we keep one this time?" Jesse pointed to the yellow pup that was busy trying to find a vacant nipple to feed on.

"Honey, we talked about this. You know we have to sell them. Besides, Mr. Clevenger might want that one to keep."

The boy hung his head. "What if I don't want to go to college?"

Amelia looked at Boone. "We started breeding Izzy when our neighbor, Ralph Clevenger, approached us because he had a registered Labrador, too. After Ralph takes his pick, I plan to sell the others and put the money in Jesse's college fund."

Boone wanted to tell Amelia that she didn't have to worry about money for college. Russ had left everything to his son, along with a hefty life insurance policy. But that wouldn't mean much to a little boy who wanted a dad. Instead, Boone spoke to Jesse. "Your mom will make sure they all have good homes with other boys and girls."

Amelia glanced down at the new mother. "This is Izzy's third litter. I usually have the vet come out to check her. That's not going to happen this time."

He could hear the worry in her voice. "They should be fine for a few days."

"I hope so." Amelia walked to the kitchen sink, then turned on the water and washed her hands and forearms. When she turned, Boone held out a clean towel for her. Even in the shadowed light, he could see her fatigue. But nothing took away from her beauty.

"I can keep an eye on Izzy," he said.

She peeked back into the pantry. "I wouldn't want anything to happen to her."

"The sofa isn't that far away. You take Jesse and at least lie down. I'll stay here."

"You need sleep, too," she said.

"Yeah, Boone," Jesse said. "Come sleep with us."

Boone glanced at Amelia and saw her uneasiness. No way was he intruding any more. "How about if I come sit with you until you fall sleep?"

Jesse let out a yelp, ran to the sofa and dove under the blankets.

Boone followed, but added more logs to the dying fire before heading to the opposite sofa. With the heater running, the room was warmer. Boone sat down and looked across the large coffee table as Amelia tucked her son under the covers, then she moved to the opposite end and took off her boots. She lay back, her brown hair spread against the pillow, making him think about anything but sleep.

"Good night, Boone," Jesse said on a yawn.

Boone jerked his gaze away. "'Night, Jesse." He shut off the lantern, leaned his head against the high-backed sofa and closed his eyes. Just for a minute, he told himself.

The wind howled outside, the cracking of the warm fire combined with the boy's soft snores was like a symphony. The feel of Amelia's presence, so close but so untouchable, made him ache. He shifted, trying to push away any wayward thoughts. He didn't even know this family twelve hours ago. They didn't know him either, but that didn't seem to matter.

Amelia woke up surprised to see it was daylight. Suddenly thoughts of last night ran through her head.

The blizzard. Izzy! Snowed in with a stranger.

She sat up to see she was alone. The scent of coffee teased her nose as muffled voices came from the kitchen. No doubt it was Jesse and Boone. She glanced at the clock on the mantel. Eight-fifteen!

She got up and walked to the window. Looking out at the beautiful winter scene, she tried to gather her thoughts. A mountain of snow covered everything. She could barely see the barn, and Boone's truck was buried up to the bumper. At least it had stopped snowing. She glanced at the threatening gray sky. For now.

How long before it started again? Would they be able to plow the roads? Restore the power? Get her truck?

Suddenly the isolation bothered her even more. She and Jesse were here with a stranger. A man she was drawn to. In the last twenty-four hours, she'd been thinking about Boone Gifford instead of her grandmother's heart procedure. It was today, and she couldn't even find out how Ruby was doing.

Had Kelley tried to call her? With the utilities out, her sister would be worried about not being able to reach them. Had the storm knocked out power in Helena? She shook her head. She had to stop worrying. Kelley could handle Gram.

Laughter came from the kitchen and she smiled. At least Jesse was happy to be snowed in with a stranger.

And so was she.

Boone wasn't much of a cook, but he could whip up some scrambled eggs when he had to. And this morning he had a good reason. Jesse needed to eat, and so did Amelia. She'd already provided him with two meals yesterday. It was his turn. Besides, with the electricity on only periodically, he wasn't sure how long the food would stay fresh.

He set a plate on the table in front of Jesse. "Here you go, bud."

The boy smiled. "Thanks." He took a big bite. "Why did you call me bud?"

"It's just a friendly term. Short for buddy."

Those brown eyes widened. "I like you calling me that." The boy scooped up a forkful and took a big bite. "This is good."

Boone sat down across from Jesse and began his meal. After a minute the boy had more questions. "Boone, do you think it will stop snowing before Christmas?"

"I expect so. I'm not an expert, but it will probably stop in a few days."

"Oh." Jesse looked disappointed.

"You don't want it to stop?"

Jesse shook his head. "I want you to stay here."

The boy climbed off his chair and went to a calendar hanging on the wall that revealed the month of December, with big *X*s marked through half of the days. "See, we have eleven days before Christmas. I don't want you to leave."

"Jesse, I can't stay until Christmas."

"But what about my wish? And I wrote Santa."

Boone had no idea how to answer him. "I just happened along, bud. I have to go back to Texas."

Tears blurred the boy's eyes. "Who's going to help me cut down a tree?"

Lost childhood memories flashed into Boone's head. He and his dad used to do that while his mother was home cooking. He blinked and focused on Jesse. "You cut down your own Christmas tree?"

The boy nodded and wiped his eyes. "Yeah, Gram, Mom and Aunt Kelley and me. This year Mom said I'm old enough to use the saw. What are we going to do if it doesn't stop snowing?"

"It's going to stop." He hoped that was true. "And you'll get your tree."

"Oh, boy, can you help us this year?"

"Can Boone help us do what?"

They both turned to see Amelia stroll into the kitchen. She was wearing the same jeans and sweatshirt, now wrinkled from sleep. Her hair was mussed and hung against her shoulders.

"Hi, Mom." He went flying across the room and hugged her. "Boone said you were tired and we should let you sleep. He fixed me breakfast, and he can help us cut down a tree." The boy finally took a breath.

Her gaze met Boone's and she smiled. He felt it all the way into his gut.

"Looks like you two have been making a lot of plans. Did you also happen to notice all the snow?"

"When it stops we can go," Jesse said hopefully. "Boone said we have plenty of time before Christmas."

Boone couldn't stop the boy's excitement, or his heart racing as Amelia looked at him.

All he managed was a nod at the coffeemaker. "Coffee?"

"Please," she said. "I think I'm going to need it." She followed him to the counter. He filled a mug and handed it to her. Close up her eyes were dark from sleep.

"I brewed some coffee while the generator was on."

She took a sip and sighed. "So worth it." Her gaze met his, then glanced away. "It has stopped snowing, but probably not for long."

He wasn't happy about the forecast. "So there's no hope that it will warm up today and melt the snow?"

She smiled and his heart tripped again. "Getting cabin fever?"

"I did get out to the barn," he told her. "Had to do a little shoveling to get there."

Amelia's son jumped into the conversation. "Boone wouldn't let me go with him. I had to promise to stay here." The boy smiled. "I got to watch the puppies, so Izzy could go outside and do her business."

Amelia tried to keep her focus on Jesse, but having Boone in her kitchen was definitely a distraction. Especially a man who handled chores and could cook breakfast.

"Thanks for your help, honey. Why don't you finish your breakfast before it gets cold?" She expected an argument, but Jesse only walked back to his seat.

She had no choice but to acknowledge Boone. "Thank you for letting me sleep."

He shrugged. "I didn't see any reason to wake you. You were sleeping so soundly."

She took another sip. "How did the horses do last night?"

"They were fine. Happy for a little attention."

She leaned against the counter and watched her son eat. "Kelley usually handles their care. But someone had to take Gram for her procedure." She frowned. "I just wish I knew how the procedure went. If everything went well, they should come home tomorrow." She glanced out the window. "That isn't going to happen, either."

Boone knew that if Kelley Hughes came home, she'd discover he wasn't the ranch hand she'd hired. He used that rationalization for not telling Amelia the truth. Right now, she needed his help. With another winter storm coming, they seemed destined to stay together. But he still needed to tell her the reason for his visit, and soon.

But he still wanted to ease her mind. "Do you have a cell phone?"

She nodded. "It's funny, but there's poor reception inside the house." She went into the other room then returned with her phone. "No service."

"Your grandmother is in the best place possible. If this storm came any earlier she could have been stranded here and unable to get the care she needed."

Amelia nodded. "I know you're right, but it doesn't stop me from worrying. She's my family. Gram raised Kelley and me. Jesse, too. She's our rock. She wasn't too keen on having the procedure. Somehow Kelley talked her into it." She smiled. "Kelley's a little more forceful than I am."

"So you three run this place?"

"Yes. A mama-and-baby cattle operation, and a yearling herd in the summer. We lease some of the grazing land and rent out three cabins during hunting season."

"That's a lot for three people to handle."

"It didn't start out that way. When we were little, our parents moved here to work in the cattle business. Mom died shortly after I was born, and we were barely settled here when Dad was thrown from his horse. He was in a coma for a while, then he eventually died.

"Grandma Ruby and Granddad Jesse stepped in and raised us. Then about six years ago, Granddad died. Gram said we had no choice but to go on."

Amelia drew a breath and released it, but he could still see her pain as she looked at him. "What about you, Boone Gifford? You said you were buying a place in Texas. Where?"

He drank the rest of his coffee. "Outside of Odessa, Texas. It had been my family's place, but when my parents passed away, I couldn't make a go of it on my own. Now I have a little more capital to carry me through the rough times. I'm hoping to buy the ranch back from the bank."

"There sure are enough foreclosures around here," Amelia added. "Is there anyone else back there to help you?"

He shook his head. There had been someone once, until he lost everything, but he didn't want to talk about the past. "It's just me." He suddenly realized how sad that sounded.

CHAPTER SIX

BOONE STARED OUT the kitchen window as night began to fall on his second day trapped with Amelia Hughes. Again flurries started blowing against the window, letting them know that another storm was brewing. He'd hoped that if the weather held tonight, he could take off tomorrow. Only, that meant he'd be leaving Amelia and Jesse to fend for themselves.

He couldn't do it.

That was the excuse he'd given himself all day to keep from mentioning Russ's name and handing over his friend's personal things. Worse, it would mean spoiling a little boy's Christmas.

Instead he'd kept the fireplaces going, fed the stock just as if he were the hired hand. He also occupied Jesse to keep him from being bored. It wasn't hard. He liked spending time with the boy, even with his endless questions that every kid asked.

He'd also been plagued by a different kind of guilt. If Russ hadn't hung back to save him, he might be here himself to meet his son.

Boone couldn't think about that now. He had to fulfill his promise. Somehow before he left the Rocking H Ranch, he had to find a way to tell Amelia the truth about his connection to Jesse's father.

He glanced at Amelia. Earlier he'd made it out to the barn to check on the animals. The temperature had risen some during the day, but after hearing the forecast on the radio, he had no doubt they were in for more snow. So that meant he had to stay put for now.

He got up from the kitchen table while Jesse set up another game for them and went into the living room to find the beautiful brunette pacing. Tall and graceful, Amelia reminded him of a Thoroughbred with her fine bones and delicate features.

Were the men around here blind? Even after only a few days together, she was going to be hard to leave.

"Amelia," he called to her.

She turned around. "What?"

"Worrying isn't going to help."

She seemed to relax a little and offered him a hint of a smile. "I know." She sighed. "I guess I'm the one with cabin fever now."

"It's understandable."

"We haven't had a bad storm like this for a few years. I guess we're overdue." She looked out the window at the fading light. "I normally love this time of year. It's beautiful here with the mountains covered in snow." She raised her startling green eyes to his. "I guess I miss Kelley and my grandmother, too. What if something has happened to Gram, and Kel can't reach me?"

He shook his head. "You can't think that way. From what you've said about her, she's a strong woman."

A smile appeared on her pretty face. "Yeah, she is. We had to fight to even get her to go to the hospital. And the doctor said she was healthy enough to handle this procedure."

"See. She's strong like I said."

"You have to be when you run a ranch."

Amelia enjoyed talking with Boone. She didn't get much male companionship, and she never realized how much she missed it. And she had to admit, it was nice to lean on someone for a change. Just so she remembered that he was doing a job, and he'd be leaving for Texas soon. If she were looking for something serious, Boone wasn't the man. He wasn't even from around here. And Montana was her home.

Besides, she wasn't sure she could trust a man again. That foolish girl who'd been willing to run off with the first guy who'd given her attention no longer existed. She was a mother now and had to think about her child. No matter how attached

Jesse was getting to Boone, she had to make him understand that the ranch hand wasn't staying around.

His voice broke into her thoughts. "It's nice you have your family."

She nodded. "They've both been there for me and my son."

"From what I gather from Jesse, his dad hasn't been in his life."

Amelia never explained her life to strangers. She'd never needed to before. "It's no secret that I never married Jesse's father. When Russ found out I was pregnant, he took off. Never heard from him again."

"You must have been pretty young."

She glanced away. "And naive. It's funny how easy it is to let love cloud your judgment. Yet, at nineteen, I'm not sure we even know what it is."

"Love can do that to you."

Something in his low tone of voice caused her to turn around. "Sounds like you have your own experiences."

He shrugged. "Past history. I found out in time."

Amelia could see a flash of hurt. She wanted to reach out to him, but she held back. "Were you married?"

His dark eyes met hers. "No, but we planned to, before I lost the ranch."

"She left you?"

His jaw tightened. "I don't blame her. I didn't have anything to offer her."

"Don't say that. You had love. She should have stood by you. Together you could have worked to get it back. That's what love is, working for a future." She crossed her arms. "Well, you're lucky to be rid of her."

An easy smile crossed his face. "You are fierce when riled. Remind me never to cross you."

"I'm sorry. It just seems that so many people just walk away when things get too rough. A commitment means sticking it out through the hard times as well as the good times." She blinked at the sudden tears welling in her eyes. "You had to be devastated, losing your home, then someone you love. I'm sorry." She moved away, swiping at the rush of tears. "I don't know what's wrong with me."

He touched her arm. "No, Amelia. Please, you have no reason to be sorry." He came closer. "Besides, it was a long time ago. I don't think about Kendra anymore."

"Good. She doesn't deserve your time."

"God, Amelia. I wish…"

His dark gaze held hers, and Amelia knew it could be trouble. She wanted to blame what she was feeling on the storm and their being thrown together.

"If only I had met someone like you," Boone began.

"Yeah, right. A single mother with a child. Not that I've been pining after Russ after all these years. I haven't. It took a while, but I realized I don't need a man to make me complete. Of course, that doesn't mean men are exactly beating down my door."

"Then, they aren't worth your time. And they sure don't deserve you. If things were different—"

Amelia held up a hand. She didn't need to hear his reasons why he couldn't be that man. "It's okay, Boone."

She started to move away, but he stopped her. "I was about to say there are things you don't know about me. And there's also the fact that you live in Montana and I live in Texas."

Three hours later Boone was in his room. Restless, he'd done a fifteen-minute workout, hoping exhaustion would help him sleep. He should be used to the confinement after living and working on the oil platform, except there he had television and other guys to talk to.

All he had here was a five-year-old boy and one beautiful woman, making him realize what was missing in his life. And tonight he nearly stepped over the line. Just touching Amelia's softness had him reeling with need. It had taken everything in him to keep from dragging her into his arms and kissing her senseless. Great, he was turning into some sex-starved maniac.

Boone suddenly heard the puppies' cries. He hurried to the pantry, hoping they hadn't woken up anyone else in the house. Amelia was already there. She was leaning over the box. He started to move away, but she turned toward him.

"Seems they want some attention." She stroked the tiny animal in her hands.

Boone couldn't resist and sank down beside her, trying not to notice as his leg rubbed against hers. He scratched Izzy's head, then gently scooped up one of her crying babies. "You know, you're spoiling them," he told her.

"Everyone needs some spoiling. Besides, I don't get to keep them long. All these precious babies will be in other homes soon."

He smiled down at the now-sleeping chocolate-colored pup. He wouldn't mind having one of these himself. He shook away the thought. It would be another connection to Amelia Hughes, and give him a reason to keep in touch. She probably wouldn't want to when she learned the truth about him.

Amelia propped her back against the shelves that stored canned goods. Boone did the same on the other side. Even though the small closet was cold, it wasn't bad, or was it the fact she warmed his blood whenever she got near him?

"Jesse asleep?" he asked.

She nodded. "He fought it for a long time, but lost in the end. Thank you for helping burn off some of his energy earlier."

"He does seem to have a lot to burn, doesn't he?"

"Always had." Amelia smiled as if she were remembering. "Even as a baby. He crawled at five months, and was walking before he was a year old." She continued to stroke the puppy. "I guess I should say running. He hasn't stopped since."

"He's a fine boy, Amelia. Any man would be proud to have him for a son."

"Thank you." Her smile faded. "There are times when I think I've cheated Jesse, with him not having a father."

This was the time he could tell her. "Earlier you said the boy's father was never in his life. Have you explained why to Jesse?"

She shook her head, but didn't seem angry at the question. "Somewhere around the age of four he began asking about his daddy. I only told him that he lived somewhere else. Then this year he went off to kindergarten and discovered all the other kids had fathers." She glanced at him. "That's how this silly Christmas wish came about. A little girl on the school bus, Emma Clark, told him to make a wish for one. Jesse took it to heart." She released a long breath. "I don't know what's going to happen when Christmas arrives and he has to face reality."

"It's a hard lesson for a little boy. I wish…" He hesitated and looked at her. "I wish things could be different."

She smiled and his gut tightened with longing.

"You know what they say," she began "'If wishes were horses, beggars would ride.'"

He nodded, silently cursing Russ for putting him in this spot, and for waiting so long to contact his son. Now it was too late, and Boone had to bring the bad news to a little boy. "I know I won't be around much longer, but if you ever need anything for the boy, you can call me."

Amelia was shocked by Boone's offer. It also made her look at reality, too. He'd be going back to Texas. "Oh, Boone, that's sweet of you, but we can't intrude on your life. Besides, you'll be so far away."

"Not that far." He put the pup back with its mother.

Amelia couldn't stop looking at his hands. His palms were large and his fingers long and tapered. What would they feel like against her skin? A shiver ran down her spine. She shook away the thought. "But you'll have your own life."

"I doubt I'll have time for a life if I'm busy with a ranch." He shrugged, his gaze focused on her. "A boy needs a man around when he gets to a certain age." Then hurried on to say, "That's not to say you won't find someone, you're very attractive. But if you don't, then you can always call me."

Amelia's heart pounded as she put her pup back with Izzy, then bravely leaned forward and planted a chaste kiss on Boone's cheek. She pulled back slightly and swallowed hard. "You're a sweet man, Boone Gifford."

The look in his eyes quickly changed as the irises darkened to a smoldering black. "You wouldn't say that if you knew what I was thinking right now." His voice was low and husky.

Amelia knew she should get out of there, but it had been so long since she'd been close to a man. A man who stirred her. A man who made her yearn to feel his touch, his kiss.

She threw caution to the wind and said, "Tell me, Boone."

He didn't hide his surprise, as he reached out and cupped

her face. "Can't seem to find the words, darlin'. I'll show you," he breathed as his mouth closed over hers.

The kiss was gentle at first, but it still sent Amelia's heart racing, as she hoped and prayed that he would never stop. Her hopes were answered as he pulled her against him and deepened the connection. His tongue slid along her lips until she opened for him, letting him inside to caress and taste her. With a moan she wrapped her arms around his neck and used her tongue to tease him.

On a groan, his hand moved to her breasts, stroking their fullness. He broke off the kiss, his gaze searching her face. Neither spoke as he dipped his head and kissed her again and again. She'd never known such hunger, such need. She'd kissed men since Russ, but it had never felt like this.

Boone's hand slipped under her sweater, touching her skin, raising goose bumps as he reached her bra and managed to unhook the lacy garment. On a whimper, she arched her back as his masterful hands began to stroke and knead her breasts.

"Oh, Boone," she gasped.

He ran kisses down her neck, his breathing heavy. "You want more?" His fingers toyed with her nipple, causing it to tighten into a hard nub. He quickly moved to the other.

"Please," she said.

Suddenly a whimpering sound broke them apart. Izzy was standing next to them.

Boone released her. "Looks like someone else needs our attention."

"I better let her out," Amelia said as she stood.

"No, I'll do it." Boone was out of the pantry before Amelia could say anything.

Five minutes later Boone cursed at himself while he gathered wood as he waited for Izzy to finish her business. What had he been thinking? Apparently, he hadn't been thinking at all when he'd kissed Amelia Hughes. And the last thing he needed to do was fall for this woman. In the end she was going to hate him.

The chocolate lab was easy to spot in the snow. "You ready to go back inside, girl?" In answer the dog bounded up the steps. Boone wasn't as eager to return, knowing he was lying to a woman he was crazy about. He'd lost her before he'd even had a chance to win her.

CHAPTER SEVEN

THE NEXT DAY it was cold and gloomy. The snow had stopped, and all Amelia wanted to do was get out of the house. She wasn't used to being confined for so long. Maybe it wouldn't be so bad if she could hear from Kelley.

She'd listened to the news on the radio and discovered the storm had crippled the entire area, including Helena. Luckily, the weather system was moving on. Now if it would warm up enough so the snow would melt.

She wanted work crews to restore electricity and phone service. Then Boone Gifford could go back to the Sky High Ranch and things would get back to normal. She glanced at the man seated at the kitchen table with Jesse. The same man she'd kissed last night. The same man whose sure hands had caressed her skin, teasing her with a taste of pleasure she'd never experienced before. She bit back a moan of frustration.

"Mom? Are you okay?"

She fought at hiding a blush. "I'm fine, honey. Just tired of being inside."

The boy's brown eyes widened. "Boone said if it's okay with you, and I dress warm, I can go to the barn with him when he feeds the horses."

Amelia stole a glance at the man she'd been avoiding all morning. He acted as if she was the last person he wanted to be around.

Before she could respond Boone stood. "If you're worried,

you're more than welcome to come, too." His gaze met hers. "I expect we're all a little stir crazy."

She nodded. "Yes, I am. I'd be happy to have the electricity back on, too."

"I like it this way," Jesse said. "I don't have to go to school. I get to stay here with Boone."

Amelia was surprised by his statement. "I thought you liked school."

"I do. But I like staying here, too. I like Boone here, too."

"But I can't stay much longer, bud," Boone told him. "I'd planned to be back in Texas soon."

Jesse's head snapped up. "Before Christmas?"

Boone was caught between a rock and a hard place. No matter how he answered he couldn't make them both happy. "I haven't decided yet."

"We still have a while before the holidays," Amelia said.

"But what about getting a tree? Even Gram said we need to have a tree for Christmas. She promised."

"Jesse, I can't promise anything right now. Not until I hear from Aunt Kelley. Gram may need special attention when she gets home."

Boone couldn't handle the boy's disappointment. "I'll tell you what, Jesse. I won't leave until we cut down the tree."

"You mean it?"

Boone glanced at Amelia, seeing her surprise.

Grinning, Jesse got up and came around the table to hug him. "Thank you, Boone. Can we get one today?"

A funny feeling erupted in Boone's gut as the boy's arms came around him. He looked at Amelia as she folded her arms across her chest, cocked an eyebrow and waited for his answer.

"Not today. If the weather holds up, maybe tomorrow."

"Yippy," the boy cried as he ran out of the room.

Boone finally turned to Amelia. She looked beautiful this morning. Her dark hair was pulled back into a ponytail, and her face was scrubbed clean. She took his breath away. That was the main reason he had to get out of here. She was too tempting. And he'd fallen into that temptation last night.

"You shouldn't make promises you can't keep," she said.

"I'm not. Unless you have a problem with me taking him to cut down a tree?"

"Not if I go with you."

"Of course you're welcome. I just figured it's the least I could do."

She seemed angry. "You don't owe anything to my son—or to me."

Yes, he did. "It's hard not to care about the boy." He stood and came toward her. "It was you I didn't expect. I never should have crossed the line last night. I apologize. And I don't want you to feel as if you have to worry about it happening again."

She swallowed. "You have feelings for me?"

He blinked and inhaled her sweet fragrance. "Yeah, if things could be different…" He let the words trail off. "You don't need to worry, though, I'll be gone soon."

She started to say something when Jesse ran into the room. "Mom, I put on my long johns and heavy pants."

"Good," she said, then looked at Boone. "Give me twenty minutes to put on the leftovers from last night."

"We can wait," Boone said, and watched her walk out to the mud room and the freezer.

Luckily, they'd been able to store food out there. And with a propane stove, Amelia had still been able to cook. Hell, she'd come up with some pretty elaborate meals. Even dessert.

He thought about when he went back to Texas. He'd be fending for himself. And he'd be alone. No child's laughter, no woman's touch. Amelia's softness was part of who she was. It was natural for her to stroke her son's hair, kiss him or laugh easily at something he said.

Thoughts of last night came rushing back with a jolt. Her kisses that had him so turned on he couldn't think, only feel. But there was a big possibility that she wouldn't want anything to do with him when she learned his secret. So he had to keep thinking of her as off-limits.

Amelia came back from the freezer carrying a large plastic container and a pie wrapped in heavy plastic. With a smile, she held up her findings. "I also found a pie. Apple. And I'll make some biscuits."

"Sounds great," he agreed. Everything around here was great. So much so he never wanted to leave. But he had to. He knew he'd never be welcome here once he told her why he'd come.

Amelia followed closely behind Boone, who'd taken charge of Jesse as they trekked through the snow toward the barn. Her son was busy asking a dozen questions.

She wanted to tell him to stop, but knew the child had been so good over the past few days of being stuck indoors. And Boone was the reason for that. The man had the patience of a saint to put up with an inquisitive five-year-old.

They reached the large door, and Boone rolled it back just enough for them to get through. Once inside, he closed it, and they stomped the snow off their boots. Luckily, there was sunlight coming in through a window up in the loft, helping them find their way around. Boone also turned on his large flashlight.

The familiar scent of horses and manure assaulted her nose. She didn't mind it at all. This was her life and she loved living out here.

"I think I better muck out some stalls," she said as she went to turn on a few of the battery lanterns next to the stalls.

"I'll help, Mom."

"No need," Boone said.

"We'll all help." Amelia turned to her son. "Right, Jesse?"

The boy nodded, went to the first stall and climbed up on the slats to pet the red roan gelding. "This is the horse I ride, Spitfire. I call him Fire." He rubbed the horse's nose. "He was grandpa's horse, but he died before I was born."

The boy continued with his introductions. "That's Penny. She's Mom's." He pointed to the stall across from them. "And that's Risky. He's Aunt Kelley's horse. Mom says she's going to break her neck someday because he's crazy."

Boone walked across the aisle to the large chestnut gelding. He had a feeling this horse matched Kelley Hughes perfectly. "He's a good-looking animal." Boone rubbed the horse's muzzle.

Amelia came over, too. "He's got a little too much attitude for me."

"That's what Aunt Kelley likes." Jesse climbed down from the stall railing. "She says Risky keeps her on her toes."

Amelia smiled. "Or her bottom," she murmured. "How many times has this horse bucked her off?"

Jesse laughed. "I'm gonna tell her you said that."

Amelia gave an exaggerated gasp. "You're such a traitor. Okay, what's it gonna cost me to keep you quiet?"

He gave her a sheepish grin. "Chocolate brownies."

Amelia placed her hands on her hips, continuing the game. "My Peppermint Kiss Brownies?"

"Sprinkled with crushed candy canes."

She turned to Boone and cocked an eyebrow. "And will that buy your silence, too?" she asked, including him, too.

"Say yes, Boone," Jesse begged. "They're her special Christmas brownies."

His gaze connected with Amelia's. He wouldn't mind her sweetening the deal with a few kisses. "I can be bought."

Amelia seemed to be just as mesmerized. "I have to check to see if I have all the ingredients. If not, I'll have to wait to make a trip to town."

Boone nodded, knowing he wouldn't be around to sample them, or a lot of other things he'd come to like since he'd been here. "I better get to work."

He turned toward the feed bin, and Jesse followed him. Amelia, on the other hand, went for the wheelbarrow and pitch fork and headed for Penny's stall to clean it.

He wanted to stop her, but he knew that women and men shared the chores on a ranch. Especially women who didn't have a man around. For a second, he let himself think about staying. Then he quickly dismissed the idea. After learning of his deception, Amelia Hughes wouldn't want him here.

"Come on, bud. Let's hurry so we can help your mom."

It took just minutes to feed the animals, but mucking out the stalls took a lot longer. Once fresh straw was spread out and water buckets filled, they were pretty much finished for the day.

Jesse followed Boone outside. After clearing a spot of snow, they dumped the barn waste. But before heading back to the house, the boy pointed to the grove of pine trees about two hundred yards away that covered the hillside.

"See, Boone, that's where we go to get our tree."

"That's not too far, Jesse."

"Then can we go and find a tree?"

"The problem is, bud, we can't get there. The snow is still too deep."

The child jerked his cap-covered head around to his mother. "Mom, can we go on the snowmobile?"

Amelia looked thoughtful, then said, "I guess we could."

"Have you ever driven a snowmobile, Boone?"

He shook his head. "There's no need in Texas."

She turned back to her son. "Let's give the weather one more day, Jesse. Tomorrow if the weather holds. Maybe."

The boy couldn't hide his disappointment as they all trudged back to the house.

"You don't have to do this, Boone," Amelia said softly. "Cutting down a tree wasn't part of your job description."

"It's not a problem, Amelia." The snow crushed under their booted feet as they measured each slippery step. Their bodies brushed in the narrow path.

Amelia spoke first. "There are more immediate things to deal with than a Christmas tree."

"Not to a little boy." He studied her profile, her pert nose and rosy cheeks. Her lips looked a little chapped, and he wondered if it was from the cold, or his kisses. "So, if it isn't a problem for you, I wouldn't mind going out tomorrow."

"It's not a problem." She turned to him, and suddenly lost her balance. He reached out and grabbed her, pulling her against him. Even through their heavy clothing, he felt her warmth, her softness.

"You should be careful," he said. "You could hurt yourself."

Their gazes held for what seemed to be an eternity. He couldn't do anything to stop the urge to lean forward and kiss her. He nearly did, but then they heard Jesse call.

"Mom, the phone rang. It's Aunt Kelley."

"Tell her I'm coming." She scrambled to break away and carefully made her way to the house.

Boone hung back. This could be it if Kelley informed Amelia that he wasn't the man hired to help out. He glanced toward his truck, still half-buried in snow. Even if he dug it out, he doubted he could handle the unplowed roads.

He continued the trip to the house and went inside in time to see Amelia hang up the phone. She turned and he saw the tears in her eyes.

He went to her. "What happened?"

She shook her head. "Nothing. Gram is fine. She just came out of surgery a few hours ago. They held it off until today. Because of the storm, the hospital only took care of emergency cases until electricity was restored." A smile broke out. "She's going to be fine. The angioplasty went great. And obviously the phones are back up."

"That's wonderful. So they'll be coming home soon."

"Kelley said it wouldn't be for a few days."

Jesse stepped in. "Then tomorrow we can get the tree and surprise Gram Ruby."

"It's still up to Boone."

They both looked at him. There had been a lot he couldn't do because of the situation, but he wasn't going to disappoint a boy at Christmas.

"We'll find a way to do it."

CHAPTER EIGHT

LATER THAT NIGHT Boone stood at the window, looking out at the brightly lit yard that allowed him to see all the way to the barn. The electricity had been restored just hours ago. Tomorrow the forecast was for sunny skies and warmer temperatures. That meant roads would soon be cleared and he could leave, but not before he finished his business here.

First, he had to keep a promise to a little boy and cut down a tree. He smiled, realizing he was looking forward to it himself. How long had it been since he'd had a Christmas tree? Since he'd celebrated the holidays, for that matter?

He flashed back to his childhood and his parents' ranch. How his mother had decorated the house for the holidays. They'd never had much money, but she always came up with some kind of special gifts.

Seeing Jesse's enthusiasm reminded him of the things every kid should have. A happy Christmas. The boy had a lot, except for a dad, but that was what he wanted most of all.

For a split second Boone thought about Jesse's Christmas wish. The idea was farfetched, maybe he was even crazy to think he could fill the spot as the five-year-old's dad. Yet he couldn't stop thinking about it. Or about Amelia.

Boone drove his fingers through his hair. She was a beautiful woman who kept him awake at night. It wasn't just her beauty that drew him, she had strength and courage. His gut tightened as he thought about the way she looked at him with those rich-green eyes. He felt his body stir as he recalled her hands on him. Damn, he was halfway in love with her already.

"Boone."

He swung around to see Jesse dressed in pajamas. "Hi, kid. Looks like you're ready for bed."

"Yeah, Mom's making me sleep in my room."

Amelia appeared from the kitchen. "I think we all need a good night's sleep. Besides, you get to watch your favorite video."

"I know," he said. "I want to say good-night to Boone, first." Before Boone realized what the boy intended, he came to him and hugged him around the waist. "'Night, Boone."

Boone placed his hands on the boy's shoulders, and his chest tightened. "'Night, bud, see you in the morning."

Jesse pulled back and looked up at him with big brown eyes. "And we're going to find a tree tomorrow?"

"I'm planning on it."

The boy rewarded him with a big grin. "Okay!" He took off and ran up the stairs.

Boone turned to find Amelia smiling at him. "It's still okay to go, isn't it?"

"Yes." She walked toward him.

His heart raced as she drew closer, then reached up and planted a kiss on his cheek. He wanted to pull her into his arms but resisted and remained still.

She pulled back. "Thank you," she whispered, then turned and followed after her son.

"You're welcome," he breathed as she disappeared upstairs. He blew out a breath. Okay, maybe he was all the way in love with her. What made it worse, he knew she had feelings for him, too. But after tomorrow, when he told her the truth, would she still have those feelings?

The next morning the weather was brisk but sunny. Bundled up in heavy coats, scarves and gloves, Amelia led the group out to the shed. After clearing away the snow, Boone slid the door open and they went inside. The two brightly painted snowmobiles were fairly new and well cared for, Boone concluded, as he put a small hand saw and some rope into the compartment.

Amelia gave Boone some basic instructions, then went to her sled. Jesse climbed on behind his mother and she looked over her shoulder. "We're not going to cut down a huge tree, Jesse," she said. "Let's keep it between six and seven feet."

"How tall is that?" the boy asked.

"Just a little taller than me," Boone said as he climbed on the other vehicle, started it, then drove out of the shed. He rode around the yard, getting a feel for the machine. Amelia, with Jesse onboard, led the way over the deep-packed snow. The trip didn't take long, as they stopped a few hundred yards from the house.

Boone climbed off, but instead of looking at the trees, he glanced back at the compound. The sprawling green house with white shutters, the red barn with a circle of fencing around the corral. It reminded him of a Christmas card.

"Is something wrong?"

He shook his head. "No. It's just about perfect. This is incredibly beautiful."

Amelia's expression showed her pride. "I've always thought so," she said. "Worth putting up with an occasional blizzard. You should see it in the spring. It's so lush and green."

He could only imagine. "How large is your place?"

She pointed toward the mountain range. "About seven sections. To the foothills in the west, and to the south we border the Sky High Ranch. The Anderson place is to the east. It's been up for sale this past year. Kelley would like to buy it, if only for the water and prime grazing land. The price is a steal, but we don't have the capital right now."

For a brief moment he allowed himself to think about what would happen if he decided to stay here and bought the Anderson place. He quickly shook off the idea. Texas had always been where he'd called home.

"Hey, Mom. Boone."

They both turned to see Jesse already on the search. He was standing beside a huge pine.

"Is this too big?"

Boone marched through the snow. "Let me see, bud." He stood next to the eight-foot-plus tree. "I think we'd have some trouble getting this one into the house."

He glanced at Amelia to see her smiling at him, and he had trouble concentrating on finding a tree. Every time he glanced in her direction, she seemed to be watching him.

When Boone helped Jesse up the steep slope, he suddenly felt a thud against his back. He turned and found Amelia packing another snowball between her hands. Without hesitation she threw it at him. He ducked just in time.

Boone smiled. "Hey, are you trying to start something?"

"Just thought I'd introduce you to a Montana pastime. You don't get any chances like this in Texas. I bet you don't even know how to make a snowball."

Before she had a chance to fire off the next one, Boone took cover behind the tree, and Jesse quickly followed him.

"Your mom's a good shot."

The boy nodded. "She's good with a rifle, too."

"That's nice to know." Boone scooped up a handful of snow and formed a ball. He stepped out to throw it and got hit square in the chest. He shot his off, but it hit the tree.

He heard the feminine laughter and smiled. "Looks like I need to show your mom I know how to play, too."

He glanced around the area. "I need to sneak up behind her. You stay here and keep throwing snowballs."

The boy grinned. "It's the boys against the girls, huh?"

"That's right." Boone took off up the hill, then circled around the trees until he ended up behind Amelia.

"Come on, Boone, come out and face me like a man," she yelled. "You, too, Jesse."

Boone came closer. "Maybe you should come out, too."

With a gasp, Amelia swung around to get off a shot. Boone was quicker, and grabbed her, trapping her loaded hand between them. "You better drop it, Amelia. You've lost."

She squirmed to get out of his hold. "Never."

He sucked in cold air to cool off the blast of heat she caused. "I guess I have to make you surrender."

"You can try, buster."

Her struggle threw them both off balance and they ended up in the snow. He landed on the bottom to cushion her fall, but he quickly reversed their positions. He looked down at the beautiful Amelia. Their eyes locked and he couldn't take his next breath. That wasn't all she caused; she made him forget all about common sense.

He groaned. "You're going to be the death of me, woman." He started to dip his head to hers when he heard Jesse's voice. Damn if he hadn't forgotten about the boy.

Boone glanced up the hill to see Jesse trudging through the snow. "Yeah, Boone, you captured Mom," he said.

He looked down at Amelia, fighting the temptation. "I guess I did, but if we're going to find a tree, I better let her go."

Boone got to his feet, then offered a hand to help her up. Once standing, she quickly turned her attention to her son.

"You know, Jesse," she said. "I saw a tree the other day that was about the right size."

"Aw, Mom. I want to pick it out this year."

She nodded. "Okay, but I thought if we got back in time, we could make a batch of Christmas cookies."

The boy's face lit up. "Well, maybe you can kind of show me where the tree is."

Amelia rubbed her hands together. "All right, let's go get a tree. It's cold out here."

Not to Boone. His body had plenty of heat. "Lead the way."

Together they made their way up the hill though the grove of trees. When Jesse gave his okay on the pine his mother found, Boone went back for the saw and rope.

Twenty minutes later they pulled up at the back door. Boone carried the tree to the porch with Jesse's help and Amelia's direction.

Next, he followed her up to the attic to carry down the tree stand and lights. Within the next hour the tree had been put in the stand and moved in front of the living room windows.

Jesse stood back and inspected the position of the tree. "Now Gram Ruby can see it when she comes home tomorrow."

After Boone had strung the lights and plugged them in, Amelia stood back with her son and admired the job. Watching this man take charge of things and interact with her son so patiently, she found just another thing to admire about him. Not that she needed any more. Even knowing he wasn't staying around, she still couldn't stop the growing attraction. Today in the snow had proved that. She wanted him to kiss her. Even his simple touch left her wanting more. It had been so long since any man made her feel like a woman.

She felt a tugging on her sweater. "Mom, can I start putting on the ornaments?"

"Sure. I'll help."

Boone climbed down from the ladder and started to leave. "I'll go check on the stock."

"No, Boone." Jesse raced to him. "Don't go!"

Boone shot a glance at Amelia. "I think this is a family tradition you should share with your mother."

"But I want you to help, too," Jesse argued.

Amelia realized that she wanted Boone to share this time, too. She held out a shiny ball. "Please, stay and help."

It was after nine o'clock that night when Amelia finally had tucked her son in his bed. For the first time in a long time, she wanted to rush the ritual. Her thoughts were on Boone as they had been every day and night since he'd come here. The man had come into their lives during a crisis, and she was going to do everything she could to get him to stay.

"Mom…"

Amelia stopped at the door. "What, honey?"

"I don't want Boone to go away."

She had expected this. She just didn't know what to do about it. "You know he lives in Texas. It's his home."

In the dimly lit room, she watched her son sit up. "Why can't he live here with us? I know he likes us. Gram Ruby and Aunt Kelley will like him, too."

She knew her sister would have doubts about any man. Amelia walked back in and sat down on the edge of the bed. "Of course he likes us, you especially."

"And he likes you, too."

Amelia felt a blush rising to her cheeks. "Well, I like Boone, too."

"Maybe you can marry Boone so he can be my dad."

She gasped, but secretly wished she could give her son what

he wanted. "Jesse, we've talked about this. You can't just wish for a dad and have him appear."

"But I did wish, and Boone did come."

"That's because Aunt Kelley hired him to help us during the storm." She brushed back hair from his forehead. "And when Kelley and Gram get home tomorrow, Boone has to leave."

"Not if you tell him you want him to stay." Big tears ran down his cheeks. "I know you like him. Please, Mom. Don't let him go away."

She pulled her child into a tight embrace as tears flooded her own eyes. "Oh, Jesse. I love you so much, and I wish I could give you what you want, but I can't. I can't give you a dad."

The boy raised his head. "Why don't you ask him?"

Boone rolled over in bed. He heard the clock on the mantel chime twice. Two in the morning. He rolled over trying to erase everything from his mind so he could get some sleep. He tossed and turned, trying to convince himself that not telling Amelia the truth was what he had to do.

He sat up. No it's wrong. He should have told her before now. Should have told Jesse about his father. Now Kelley and the grandmother were coming home tomorrow and everything was going to blow up in his face.

And Amelia would never forgive him. That meant more to him than anything. He'd come to care for her, and the boy. More than he should, but it was too late to go back. He threw back the covers, got up and slipped on his jeans and flannel shirt. Not bothering with the buttons, he opened the door and went into the kitchen.

After he checked on Izzy and her puppies to see they were okay, he took a glass from the cupboard and got a drink of water. He leaned against the counter and saw the tree silhouetted in the window. He inhaled the evergreen scent. Everything about this place felt like home. A place you could feel as if you belonged.

That yearning had eaten away at his gut. He'd spent years standing on the outside. Now that he'd gotten a taste of it, he wanted more. Every time he looked at Amelia and Jesse.

There was a creaking sound, and he turned toward the stairs to see Amelia. His heart stopped, then began to pound in his ears. He couldn't take his eyes off her as she walked across the living room. Her long robe was open and flowing around her legs. Her dark hair unbound. His fingers ached to be tangled into the thick strands.

She stopped to glance at the decorated tree, giving him the opportunity to head back to his room, but he was rooted to the spot. She continued on, but when she saw his silhouette she gasped.

"Boone?"

"Sorry, I didn't mean to frighten you."

She shook her head. "It's okay. I'm just distracted tonight." She went to the cupboard. "You're having trouble sleeping, too."

"Seems we both are."

"My reason is Jesse." She filled her glass with water. "Why can't you sleep?"

He paused for a while, then couldn't be anything but honest. "You."

In a second. Boone clenched his fists to keep from touching her.

"Besides, don't you have to give notice at Sky High?" she asked, her hands moved over him.

Boone couldn't take much more of her torture. His hands gripped her arms, but he couldn't push her away. "I need to talk to you about that." She placed another soft kiss at the base of his throat, and he was losing ground quickly.

"I think we've talked too much already."

Boone looked down at her. Her face was shadowed in the dim light, but he knew her beauty, the mesmerizing green hue of her eyes. He lost it. He pulled her into his arms as his mouth closed over hers. She made a whimpering sound and locked her fingers behind his neck.

He slanted his mouth over hers, deepening the kiss, but it still wasn't enough. He lifted her off the floor, swung around and set her down on the counter. He stepped between her legs and pulled her against him. At the same time he slipped his tongue inside her mouth and tasted her sweetness. Heaven.

He broke off the kiss and traced his lips along her jaw to her ear. "I want you so much, Amelia," he whispered. He'd never ached for a woman like this before.

"Oh, Boone, I want you, too," she cried. "Please, don't leave me. Don't ever leave me."

"Amelia." He stopped his words, not knowing how to answer her. Finally he released her, then turned away, working to regain some composure. He couldn't do this. Not until she knew the truth.

"Boone?"

He turned around. "Amelia, we need to talk." He lifted her from the counter and set her on the floor. "There's something I need to tell you. Something I should have told you when I first got here."

He led her to the table and pulled out a chair for her to sit down.

"If you don't want to be with me—"

"Don't ever think that," he interrupted, then leaned down and kissed her perfect mouth. "It's because I care about you, and Jesse, that I need to tell you the truth."

CHAPTER NINE

AMELIA NO LONGER FELT brave. She'd planned to talk to Boone when she came downstairs, even dressed in her best night-gown, in hopes of convincing him to stay. Not just for her son, but herself, too.

She sighed. "If we're going to be honest, you've been keeping me up, too."

Setting down her glass, she took a step closer and reached out to place a hand on his chest. The light atop the stove wasn't bright enough to read his eyes, but she could feel the pounding of his heart under her palm.

"Amelia, we shouldn't be doing this," he breathed.

"It feels right to me, Boone."

"We can't always go with our feelings. We have to use some common sense."

She ran her hands up his well-developed chest, and he sucked in a breath. "Sometimes that's hard to do."

"Amelia..."

She smiled, her own heart racing. "I love it when you say my name."

Boone wanted to run, but mostly he wanted to wrap Amelia Hughes in his arms and never let go. "I'm leaving in the morning."

"You don't have to. Jesse wants you to stay and so do I. There isn't any reason to rush off." She raised up on her toes and kissed the underside of his jaw. "Maybe I can even convince you to stay in Montana."

He could see her swallow. "The truth?"

Boone nodded and sank down in the other chair. "About the real reason I came here."

She blinked but didn't say a word.

"First, I don't work for the Sky High Ranch."

She stiffened. "Who are you, then, and who do you work for?"

"I am Boone Gifford like I said, and I did work on an offshore rig in Texas. That's all true. Last summer there was an accident and I got hurt." He drew a breath and released it. "That's what delayed my coming to see you and Jesse."

She gripped her hands together but didn't say anything.

"I worked with Russ Eldon."

She jumped up and went to the counter. "Russ? Russ sent you here?"

Boone stood, too. "Yes. Just listen, Amelia."

"No, Russ never wanted to be in his son's life, and he can't come here now. Not when he's denied his son all this time." She shot a hard glare at him. "Oh, God, he sent you here to cozy up to me?"

"No, Amelia, it's not like that. I only knew Russ for a few months. We both worked on the rig together, shared living quarters. He talked about Jesse."

"No, he couldn't! He didn't know about Jesse. He took off before I had my son. And he never once contacted me."

"About six months ago he found out that you had a boy. He told me he wanted to come here and meet his son. So he was trying to make some fast money to pay you for all the years of missed child support."

"I don't want Russ's money or him in our lives. I won't allow him to come here, get Jesse excited, then take off again." Amelia swiped at her tears. "It's been more than five years and he's never wanted his son before. Why now?"

"The only thing he wanted Jesse to know was that he existed."

Arms folded across her chest, she paced back and forth. "See, he couldn't even come himself. He sent you."

"He couldn't come, Amelia. Russ isn't here because he's dead."

Amelia froze. Russ was dead. She finally looked at Boone. "How?"

"In a hurricane. We were evacuating the oil platform and our helicopter crashed into the ocean. Russ was one of the three who didn't make it out. He drowned."

Amelia remembered hearing about last summer's hurricane that caused massive destruction along the Texas coast.

Boone continued the story. "Russ put Jesse down as next of kin on the insurance policy. But with the boy being a minor, he asked me to be executor if anything happened to him." He shrugged. "I never thought anything about agreeing to it. I never thought this would happen…" He paused, then said, "I would have come sooner, but I spent time in the hospital, then a rehab facility until recently."

"You were injured?"

He nodded. "My back and shoulder. I needed surgery and therapy."

She glanced over his body, remembering earlier how he'd winced when he rolled over in the snow. "Are you okay now?"

"Yeah, thanks to Russ. He kept me afloat and saved my life."

The Russ she remembered had been cocky and self-centered. Tears welled in her eyes as she raised her gaze to Boone and burst into tears. Why did this have to happen now? Why had Boone deceived her?

He led her back to the chair. "I'm sorry, Amelia. I know this is hard for you—"

She pulled away from his touch. "Yes, I'm mourning Russ, but for my son, not because I have any feelings for him. I got over that girlhood crush a long time ago. The tears are for my son. For the father he never got to know. Oh, God," she cried. "How can I tell Jesse?"

"I know my timing sucks, but I came as soon as I could." He went into the bedroom and returned with an envelope. He laid it on the table. "I'm not condoning what Russ did to you and Jesse, but I know he regretted abandoning you and his son." He nodded at the package on the table. "There are a few personal effects, a letter to Jesse and the life insurance policy. I signed it over to you."

She didn't touch any of it. "So I'm supposed to show my son this, as if it could ever make up for all the years Russ was never here?"

"No, of course not." He sighed. "But at least it shows your son that his father planned to be a part of his life. He wasn't perfect, none of us are, but Russ was trying."

She remained silent.

"I'll do anything I can to help, Amelia."

"I think you've helped more than enough. Jesse wants a real dad and he's nominated you for the job."

Boone shifted his feet. "I know I made a mess of this, but I care about Jesse. And I care about you."

She raised her hand. "I can't listen to this now."

"I'd planned to tell you when I arrived, but I didn't want to frighten you when we ended up trapped in the house together. Then I never found the right time."

She glared at him. "How convenient for you."

"I'm sorry, Amelia. I'll leave in the morning."

He stood, went into the bedroom and began to pack up his things. He'd only been here four days, but it seemed like so much longer. Long enough to have feelings for Amelia. And to even think about a future with her and Jessie. Now he wasn't going to get that chance.

Carrying his duffel bag, he returned to the kitchen. Amelia was still sitting at the table.

"If it's okay," he began, "I'll stay in the barn tonight, and after I feed the stock in the morning, I'll leave." He paused at the door, but she didn't turn to look at him.

"No matter what you think, Amelia, just know that I may have come here out of duty because Russ saved my life, but believe me, I've come to care about you and Jesse."

The following morning was bright and sunny, exactly the opposite of how Amelia felt. The pain of Boone's secret and reading Russ's letters had kept her up most of the night. But when Jesse came downstairs, she managed a smile as she cooked his breakfast.

"Where's Boone?" her son asked. "He said I could help him

feed the horses if the weather was nice. And it's sunny." He shoved a forkful of eggs into his mouth. "Can I, Mom?"

She sat down at the table with her coffee. "I'm not sure if Boone has the time, honey. He has to go back to Texas soon."

His truck was still here, although it had been moved closer to the barn. So she wasn't sure when he exactly planned to go back to Texas. Suddenly she got a strange ache in her stomach. She didn't want him to leave.

"But, Mom, he can't go back, yet. He promised to stay until Christmas no matter what. He just has to 'cause I've been wishing really, really hard that he can be my dad."

"Oh, Jesse." She sat down across from him at the table. "We talked about this before. You can't just wish for things and expect them to happen."

"But, Mom, you want Boone to stay here, too."

Before she could answer, the back door opened and Kelley walked into the kitchen. "We're home." She put down her bags and grinned at her sister and nephew.

Both Amelia and Jesse raced to the doorway, in time to see her grandmother Ruby helped in by Boone.

The short, sturdily built woman with steel-gray hair looked up at her escort with soft-green eyes. "What a nice young man you are." She glanced at Amelia. "Wherever did my grand-daughter find you?"

Boone smiled. "I just kind of showed up during the blizzard to help out."

Jesse rushed over to hug his grandmother. "No, Gram, Boone is my Christmas wish."

CHAPTER TEN

"ARE YOU GOING TO TELL ME what's been going on?" Kelley Hughes asked as she marched into the kitchen.

Amelia looked over her shoulder at her tall, trim, older sister. Kelley had long, blond hair pulled back in her usual no-nonsense braid. Her pretty face was sprinkled with freckles caused by her time in the sun.

"I've been running the ranch during a blizzard, without electricity or a phone." She smiled, feeling the pride. "And I might add, I handled things just fine."

Kelley crossed her arms over her chest. "That's not what I'm talking about. I'm talking about Boone Gifford. Who is he?"

Amelia turned around, realizing her sister wasn't going to end this discussion. "He's a ranch hand."

"Not from the Sky High Ranch, he isn't. Their foreman called me and apologized for not sending over the help he promised. Gifford was never employed there."

"I know."

Kelley's eyes widened. "Then where did he come from?"

"West Texas."

"You let a stranger stay here in this house? Amelia, you're too trusting."

"First of all, we were in the middle of a blizzard. Secondly, he rescued me and your nephew when we got stranded on the road. Thirdly, by the time we got here, we were all stuck." She waved a hand. "What was I supposed to do? Send him out in the worst storm we've had in years?"

"Of course not." Kelley glanced into the living room at the decorated tree. "But it seems he's made himself at home."

"What was I supposed to do, make him stay on the porch? No matter what you think, Kel, Boone was a perfect gentleman. He worked hard, too. He kept the fire going, fed the stock, even helped deliver Izzy's pups. He did everything a ranch hand would have done, and more."

"My, he sounds like he's too good to be true." Kelley continued to study Amelia, doubt in her hazel eyes.

She hated that her sister treated her as if she couldn't handle things. "Stop it, Kel. I know what you're thinking. What happened with Russ was a long time ago. I've grown up since then."

"Are you trying to tell me that nothing happened between the two of you?"

Amelia felt her cheeks warm. "I'm not a child, so stop treating me like one."

Her sister relented. "I'm sorry. But Boone Gifford is a good-looking man."

Amelia raised an eyebrow. "So you noticed."

Kelley bristled. "I also noticed that the man couldn't look at anyone but you. So why is he leaving?"

"Because he only came to Montana to tell me that Russ died."

"What?"

"That's what Boone was doing in Rebel Ridge. It seems last year Russ finally grew curious about his son." She went on to tell her sister about the accident that took his life and Boone's connection.

"And somehow I have to tell Jesse," Amelia said.

"Why? Russ never was a father to him."

"So I shouldn't tell him? Come on, Kelley, you know how many questions Jesse has asked about his dad. And the older he gets, the more he wants to know. I can't keep the truth from him."

"You can wait until he's a little older," Kelley urged, grabbed her jacket, then headed out the back door.

Amelia wiped her hands with a towel and went into the

living room. No matter when she told her son the news about his father, it would hurt him. She stared at the tree and inhaled the fresh evergreen scent that made her think of past holidays in this house. Since the death of their parents, Christmases had been a little lonely for her and Kelley. Maybe that was the reason for her older sister's protectiveness. Even with all the love their grandparents had showered on them, they were never a complete family. Amelia had always wanted something more for Jesse. Had hoped that Russ would come back someday to claim his son. Now that would never happen.

She felt the prickling of tears as she looked outside. Just then Boone walked out of the barn, carrying his bag to his truck. He was leaving. Her chest tightened as her fingers gripped the window curtain. She wanted to stop him, but she knew he'd fulfilled his obligation. Was that all she and Jessie had been to him? An obligation?

"That's one nice young man you've found."

Amelia turned around as her grandmother walked into the room. She was dressed in trousers and a starched print blouse. "Gram, you should be in bed getting your strength back."

Ruby waved a hand. "Bah, I've been in bed far too long. And quit trying to change the subject." The small-framed woman made her way to the window and nodded. "Why aren't you convincing Boone to stay?"

She wanted to, but how could she keep him from his dream? "Because his plan was always to go back to Texas and buy a ranch."

"That's a shame. It sure is nice to have a man around again." Gram sighed and got a faraway look in her eyes. "He reminds me a lot of my Jesse. Big and muscular with those dark roguish eyes and the easy grin. Oh, my, a man like that sure gets your heart apumping."

Amelia knew the feeling. She also knew Boone's touch, his kisses…

Her grandmother turned to her. "Good gracious girl, get to movin'. Or are you just going to let that man walk out of your life?"

Amelia was taken aback by her grandmother's words. "I

don't exactly have a choice, Gram. Boone's dream has always been to buy back his parents' ranch. He has to go home."

"No, he can't leave." Jesse hurried downstairs, dressed in his heavy coat and boots.

"Jesse Hughes, where do you think you're going?"

"Out to see Boone." The determined boy started toward the back door.

"Well, at least someone knows their mind," Gram said, then turned to her granddaughter. "Sometimes you have to go after what you want."

"And a mother also has to protect her child." Amelia took off after her son. Right or wrong, she was going to tell him the painful truth.

Although the weather was a lot warmer today, it was still cold. Boone had killed about twenty minutes, and he didn't have an excuse to hang around any longer. He'd checked the road conditions, and the main routes were clear. If he took off now, he could make good headway toward home.

Home? He suddenly wondered where that was. Where was his enthusiasm? Before coming here, all he'd wanted was to buy back the Last Dollar Ranch. He already had a deposit down on the place. All that was left was to sign the papers to finalize the deal. Now he wasn't sure that was what he wanted to do.

He heard his name called, and he looked at the house to see Jesse running toward him. He pushed off from the truck's fender and went to meet the boy on the shoveled path. The kid launched himself, and Boone caught him up in his arms.

Jesse's tiny arms wrapped around the neck. "Boone, you can't leave," he cried. "Please, don't go."

Boone gave the boy one last hug and set him down. That was when he saw the tears. "Aw, Jesse, you shouldn't be out in the cold." He worked the zipper on the child's jacket and wrapped the scarf around his neck. "I was going to come up to the house to say goodbye."

"But I don't want you to leave," Jesse cried.

Boone hated this. "I wish I could stay, bud, but there are things you don't understand."

The boy shook his head. "Mom told me about my real dad." Those questioning brown eyes held his. They were so much like Russ's. "She said you knew him. And that he died in the ocean."

Boone crouched down to be level with the five-year-old. "Your mother told you about your dad?"

Jesse jerked his head up and down. "Yeah, she said he's a hero."

Boone managed a nod. "Yeah, he was. He talked about you all the time, too. And he wanted more than anything to come and see you."

Jesse's eyes widened. "He really wanted to be my dad?"

"Yes, very much."

A smile broke out on Jesse's face as he swiped at his tears. "And he couldn't come to be with me so he sent you to be my dad."

Boone swallowed hard, not even knowing how to respond to that conclusion.

"Jesse Thomas Hughes."

They both looked up to see Amelia. Boone stood as she approached them. "Jesse, I think you need to go back inside. It's too cold out here."

"But, Mom, I had to stop Boone from going away."

Boone ignored Amelia's glare. "Look, Jesse, I might need to leave now for a little while, but I'll be back and we'll talk more about your dad."

"You promise?"

"Yes, I promise."

The boy hugged Boone's neck and whispered, "On Christmas."

"I'll try my hardest," Boone told him, barely holding it together. Suddenly all doubts about what he truly wanted faded, and he found himself adding, "I promise." He finally released Jesse and watched as the boy took off toward the house.

Once Jesse was out of sight, Amelia turned back to Boone. "Oh, Boone, how could you make him that promise?"

"Because I made a promise to his father. I owe Russ a debt." Boone took a step closer to her. "Look, I know Russ did you and Jesse wrong for a lot of years. But I believe he grew up and planned to do right by his son. Jesse needs to know that."

"I know you feel a duty to Jesse, Boone, but he will only be hurt when you finally go away."

Boone froze. "You believe I'm coming back here out of duty?" He searched her pretty face, those green eyes he'd come to love. "You really have no idea what I feel for you *and* your son? Or how hard it is for me to leave you both?"

Her gaze held his. "How do you feel?"

His heart lodged in his throat. "That I'd give anything not to have this between us. What brought us together could tear us apart." He reached out and pulled her into a tight embrace. "I care about you, Amelia."

"Don't, Boone." She closed her eyes momentarily. "Don't make this any harder. You're leaving for Texas."

"What if I came back?" If she just said the word, he would change his plans—his life for her.

She swallowed hard but didn't say anything.

"I'll need a little time, Amelia. There are things in Texas I need to take care of. And I need to give you time, too. Time for you and your son to absorb the news about Russ. All I ask is that you trust me. Can you do that?"

Amelia hesitated, then nodded. "Oh, Boone, I want to."

He smiled. "That's a start," he said right before his mouth closed over hers. He put everything he felt for her into the kiss. And by the time he released her, they were both swaying, and their breathing was labored.

"Give us a chance, Amelia. I'll prove to you that we can work this out."

Over the next week, Amelia found she couldn't pass a window without looking out, hoping to see Boone driving up the road. She'd never missed anyone so much. She tried to think about the way he'd kissed her, the promises he'd made to her, to Jesse. But lingering doubts made her face facts. What if he didn't return? Once back in Texas, he might have second thoughts. He might decide to buy that ranch he'd always wanted. Someplace where they didn't have blizzards.

It was Jesse she worried about most. He had her reread the letter from his dad every night. Russ's picture was in his room.

There had been times her son had become sad, but perked up when he talked about Boone coming back.

For the past week the first thing Jesse had done every morning was check another day off the calendar. Not so unusual for a child his age during the holidays, but Amelia knew he wasn't waiting for toys on Christmas morning. He was waiting for Boone.

The oven timer went off, and she went to pull the brownies out of the oven.

"Mom, are they ready?" Jesse asked.

She smiled. "Yes, and you're just in time to do your part. Did you crush the candy canes?"

"Yeah." He climbed up onto the chair at the table and held up the bag of red and white bits.

"Okay, I guess we're ready then." She enjoyed sharing this Christmas tradition with her son.

Jesse's little fingers worked awkwardly, sprinkling just the right amount on each square. "Mom, can you make these brownies every Christmas forever and ever?"

She smiled and thought about future Christmases. There might not be a Boone, but she could give him this. "Yes, we can make them every year." She kissed his cheek. "But only if you help me."

Jesse glanced toward the stove. "Good, you made a whole bunch." He looked up at her with those trusting eyes. "I want there to be enough for Boone tomorrow."

Her heart tightened. "Honey, we talked about this. Boone might not make it back for Christmas."

"But Mom, he's my Christmas wish. And he promised."

Amelia glanced toward the back door. Her sister came in, stripped off her coat and hat and hung them on a hook. "Hey, do I smell brownies?"

Jesse nodded. "Mom and me made them. But no one can have any until tomorrow."

Kelley frowned. "I have to wait that long?"

"We have to wait for Boone to get here." His job completed, Jesse climbed down off the chair. "Mom, can I watch a video?"

At Amelia's nod, the boy ran out of the kitchen. She began to clean up the mess, carrying things to the sink.

Kelley helped her. "Sounds like he's got his mind made up."

"Kelley, please. This has been a rough time for him."

"It hasn't been exactly easy for you, either." Her sister touched her arm. "I don't know Boone very well, but I know how much you and Jesse care about him. I hope it works out."

Amelia bit down on her lower lip. "I'm afraid to hope, Kel. Boone asked me to have faith that he'd be back, but I'm having trouble. After Russ left…"

Kelley hugged her sister. "Oh, Amelia, one thing is for sure, Boone isn't Russ. I believe the man is sincere." Kelley smiled. "Maybe you, too, need to make a Christmas wish."

CHAPTER ELEVEN

JUST BEFORE DAWN Christmas morning, Amelia shut off her alarm clock and sat up in bed. Sleep had eluded her most of the night because all she could think about was Boone. Since he left a week ago, she hadn't heard a single word from him. Not a phone call. Nothing. The faith she'd managed to carry the past seven days was fading now. How was she supposed to keep believing in him under those circumstances?

Closing her eyes, she released a sigh. If only she could push him out of her head. And her heart. But that wasn't likely, not when she'd managed to fall in love.

In just a matter of days—to a man she barely knew.

She stood and went to the window. The breaking dawn spread a dim light over the scene below. Snow blanketed the land, emphasizing each outbuilding on the ranch.

A perfect Christmas day…almost.

There was a soft knock on the door before it opened and Gram Ruby peered inside. "I heard you," she whispered and stepped inside. "You always were the first up on Christmas."

Amelia smiled. "Well, now I'm trying to get a head start on a certain five-year-old."

The older woman crossed the room to her granddaughter. "Or are you looking for your young man?"

"Gram, he's not my young man," she denied weakly.

"You need to have faith, Amelia. That's what love is. And if Boone says he's coming back, he'll be here."

That was Amelia's problem. "Gram, I'm afraid."

"Do you love him?" her grandmother asked.

Amelia glanced away. "I've only known him four and a half days."

Ruby smiled. "I knew your grandfather all of thirty seconds before I fell hopelessly in love with him. Of course he was handsome and a charmer, too." She took her granddaughter's hand as they walked to the bed and sat down. "Amelia, there isn't a timeline on love."

"But Boone lives so far away. And what about Jesse? He's just lost his biological father. What if Boone just feels obligated to us only because of Russ?" She sighed. "I can't make another mistake."

"Stop it, child. You didn't make any mistake. Russ was the one who chose to leave." She beamed. "And look what we were blessed with, our sweet Jesse. So don't let your past dictate your future. Give Boone a chance."

Amelia nodded. "I guess there isn't anything to worry about if Boone doesn't return."

"Oh, he'll return," Grandma predicted. "Then you'll have a lot to decide. So I should let you get to it." Ruby stood and headed for the door, then paused. "I just want you to be happy, Amelia. So don't give that up to please everyone else." With that said, the older woman left the room.

Amelia had a lot more to worry about than her own feelings. Jesse would always be her first concern. And if Boone didn't return, her son's heart would break. How would they both survive the day if Boone didn't show up?

Amelia couldn't think about that. She needed to make today special for her son. She quickly dressed in a burgundy turtleneck sweater, charcoal wool trousers and black boots. She tied her hair back into a knot, leaving bangs across her forehead. After applying some lip gloss, she headed downstairs.

In the shadowed living room, she turned on the tree lights and smiled at the dozens of wrapped presents piled underneath. Even though Jesse hadn't asked for any toys this year, she'd made sure Santa had left an electric train set.

Amelia went into the kitchen and turned on the coffeemaker. Several freshly baked pies lined the counter for today's holiday dinner. She wasn't even sure of Boone's favorite, so she'd made pumpkin, pecan and apple.

Usually Amelia cooked Christmas dinner, but this year Kelley was cooking, giving Amelia the day off. Could her sister's sudden domestic tendencies have anything to do with Mack Dennison? The restaurant owner of Mack's Kitchen had definitely caught Kelley's attention. Even though her sister had been trying to hide it, Amelia had seen the attraction between the two. Although she was a little envious, she was also happy her sister had found someone.

A sound drew Amelia's attention to the back door, and Kelley walked in. "Merry Christmas, sis." Smiling, she pulled off her gloves and stuffed them in her pockets before hanging her coat on the hook.

"Merry Christmas," Amelia answered.

"What are you doing up so early?" Kelley asked as she walked to the counter and poured a cup of coffee.

"I wanted a minute or two to myself before an excited little boy starts ripping into presents."

Kelley leaned against the counter. "Could it be you're waiting for some good-looking, Texas cowboy?"

Amelia sighed, knowing there was no reason to lie. "I'm probably crazy, but yes. I know he went to Texas, but what if he decided not to come back here?"

"I have a feeling he'll be back," Kelley told her. "Are you ready for that?"

"That's what I'm so torn about. How can Jesse and I leave here? What about Gram?" She looked at her older sister. "And you? You're our family—and this ranch is our home. We run it together." This past week she'd finally gotten up the nerve to tell her sister some of her ideas for the operation. "But I don't see any man around, asking me to go anywhere. So you're stuck with me."

"It's early yet." Kelley glanced out the window. "The sun is barely up."

"Since when have you become a Boone supporter?"

Kelley shrugged. "Maybe since I realized that the right man can change a lot of plans."

Amelia watched her sister closely, but Kelley didn't give anything away. A sudden movement outside the window caught Amelia's attention. In the quiet morning, the leftover snow was practically untouched, except for the cleared paths up the drive and the barn, peaceful and picturesque as a postcard. Then she saw the vehicle. The familiar red truck. A man in a sheepskin jacket climbed out.

Amelia blinked, feeling her heart begin to race. Boone. He came back.

"Looks like your man kept his promise."

Amelia barely heard her sister as she grabbed her coat, then ran for the door.

Boone was nervous, more so than at any time in his life. He wanted so much to be a part of Amelia's life. He wanted to make a family with her and Jesse. Today he had to convince them both how much he cared about them.

He'd contacted Kelley and told her his feelings and future plans, imploring her for help. Once she realized he loved her younger sister, she'd been more than willing to help with his plan.

When he glanced toward the porch and saw Amelia, his breath caught in his chest. Getting a better grip on the bag of presents, he started up the walk and took the steps two at a time until he stood in front of the woman he'd come to love. "Merry Christmas, Amelia."

"You're back."

His gaze locked with hers. Her green eyes searched his. "I said I would be."

She suddenly straightened. "For how long, Boone? How long before you leave this time? I'm not going to let you break Jesse's heart—"

Boone dropped his bag of gifts, pulled her into his arms and covered her mouth in a hungry kiss. After just a second of hesitation, Amelia wrapped her arms around his neck and kissed him back. Before Boone lost it altogether, he released her.

"That's the welcome I was hoping for. God, I've missed you." He pressed a soft kiss on the end of her nose. "Is Jesse up yet?"

She shook her head.

"Good." He winked. "Can we go inside and I'll tell you everything?"

Without a word Amelia turned and led him inside the kitchen. Once again he was hit with the warmth he'd felt that first time he walked into this house. He followed her into the deserted kitchen. Good. He wanted some alone time with Amelia, before he faced the rest of the family.

Amelia looked around. "Kelley was just here."

"She's probably giving me a chance to stake my claim."

She arched an eyebrow. "You've been in touch with my sister?"

He saw the flash of pain in Amelia's eyes and rushed on to say, "Only since yesterday. Remember, Kelley wasn't exactly happy about my first visit."

"Why didn't you call me?"

"I didn't want to do that until everything was finalized."

"So you bought your ranch?"

"Yes, I did."

Amelia tried to hold it together, but it was hard. "So why even come here, Boone? Just to get Jesse all excited again, then turn around and return to Texas?"

He moved closer. "What about you, Amelia? Are you excited that I came back?"

She pressed her hand against his chest. "Don't, Boone. This isn't about us. Jesse has to come first."

"I disagree. You come first, Amelia. With me, anyway. You are the reason I returned to Montana. Of course I'm crazy about Jesse, but it's you I've fallen in love with."

She gasped. "Boone."

"I hope that makes you happy?"

Yes! No! She nodded.

"Don't I get a little more than that?"

"Oh, Boone, I love you, too." She wanted this so much. "It's just that you live so far away. How can I leave my family?"

"Aw, honey, I would never ask you to leave here. That's the reason the ranch I bought is a lot closer. It's the Anderson place."

She blinked. "You bought the Andersons' ranch?"

"Yeah." He nodded. "Well as soon as escrow closes next week. Seems I can't get enough of Montana's blizzards, especially if I'm going to be snowed in with a certain green-eyed woman."

Amelia's throat suddenly went dry. "But what about your home in Texas?"

"It's just a place. I don't have any family there, just memories of a ranch lost." He took her hand. "I want a new start with you, Amelia, and with Jesse. But I'm going to need your help, too. I want you to be my partner."

Boone felt her stiffen and watched as her smile faded. He realized he wasn't saying this right. "Come on," he said as he tugged her into the living room and sat her down on the sofa in front of the tree. He took the spot next to her.

"A lot has happened in the past year." He cradled her hand in his. "I'd lost everything when I ended up on an oil rig and met Russ. He was the one who befriended me, not the other way around. Yeah, I listened when he talked about Jesse, because I was bitter over my own problems. Then when he kept me afloat in the water until help came…" He paused. "I realized what I owed him. But it was too late."

"Oh, Boone, you can't blame yourself for what happened that day."

"Why not? He had a son and he wanted to be a part of his life. I was all alone." He raised his gaze to hers. "Then I met you and Jesse. God forgive me, but I was suddenly glad I didn't die that day."

She smiled. "So am I."

"But your son lost his father."

Amelia's touch gave him the love and acceptance he needed. "No, Boone. Russ hadn't been a father to Jesse. I'm sorry he died, and I'm sorry for my son, but Russ had many opportunities to be a part of his life. You're the one who's been here for Jesse."

Boone took a calming breath. "And I want to continue being a part of his life and yours." He stood, then went down on one knee as he pulled a small velvet box out of his coat pocket.

That got Amelia's attention. He opened it, revealing a platinum band, square-cut diamond. "I know this seems fast, but we spent four twenty-four-hour days together. Four wonderful days. Most people who've known each other for months don't spend that much time together." He took the ring out of the box and held it in his hand. "Besides, I fell in love with you by the end of the first day. I want us to be partners in everything, Amelia. I love you and want you to be my wife. Will you marry me?"

"Oh, Boone." Tears flooded her eyes as she touched his cheek.

"Say yes, Mom."

They both turned to see a pajama-clad Jesse standing on the staircase. Then Amelia looked in the other direction to see Kelley and Gram standing at the kitchen entrance. Where had they come from? Even Izzy came out to greet them.

Amelia smiled as she turned back to Boone. "Are you sure you can handle all this family? I'm a package deal."

He grinned. "I'm planning on that. Do you think you can move as far away as the Anderson place?"

She shook her head. "No, but I'll move to the new Gifford Ranch. Oh, yes, Boone, I'll marry you."

He slipped the ring on her finger, pulled her to her feet and into his arms, then kissed her long and thoroughly as her family broke into cheers.

Once they broke apart, Jesse ran to hug them. He looked up at Boone. "See, you are my Christmas wish."

Boone knelt down to the little boy he'd been given the chance to raise. "I want to be more than that, Jesse. I want to marry your mother, but I also want to be your dad."

Those brown eyes widened. "For real?"

"For real," Boone assured him.

Jesse looked at his mother and she nodded.

The boy turned back to Boone. "Yeah, we're going to be a family."

Kelley and Gram rushed in, offering congratulations and hugs all around as they began the day's celebration. Then they tore into the presents and gasped at the gifts that Boone bought for everyone. He was also surprised when he opened the pair of fur-lined gloves that Amelia had given him. The two best gifts were Amelia and Jesse.

About a hour later, Kelley's Mack showed up and they disappeared into the kitchen and began preparing the holiday meal, giving Boone and Amelia time to be together. They bundled up and went outside for another Hughes tradition, to take a ride in the horse-drawn sleigh, giving Boone another look at Montana's winter wonderland. They laughed and made plans for the future. A wedding, a new home and a life together.

That evening Boone sat at the dining table with Jesse on one side and Amelia on the other. He grasped his new family's hands during the blessing. When it concluded, Jesse announced, "This is the best Christmas ever."

Amelia smiled as she continued to hold on to Boone's hand, feeling his ring on her finger. "I think we all got our Christmas wish."

Boone looked at her. "I know I got all mine."

Amelia could only agree as she smiled back. She would always be grateful for the man who came to rescue her and her son. And offered her love for a lifetime.

* * * * *

This season we bring you
Christmas Treats
For an early Christmas present Patricia Thayer would like to share a little treat with you...

Christmas is the best time of the year, and being with the one you love is what it's all about. Of course, after you add a warm fire, candles, mistletoe and a wonderful dessert, it's just about as perfect as it can get.

Here's one of my favorites:

PEPPERMINT KISS BROWNIES

Ingredients:
A regular box of brownie mix (any kind)
HERSHEY'S KISSES or chocolate drops
Crushed peppermint candy canes.

I use heart-shaped muffin tins, but you can use an 8x11 pan. Once they're filled, I push one HERSHEY'S KISS into each of the centers, or squares, then bake as directed. After they come out of the oven, sprinkle the crushed peppermint on top.

Enjoy,
Patricia Thayer

DONNA ALWARD

A Bride for Rocking H Ranch

Dear Reader,

Christmas has to be my absolute favorite time of year. Being from Canada, I love the snow, the ice-skating, tobogganing, hot chocolate and baking cookies with my children. I love snuggling in with a holiday movie, and singing along with Christmas carols. I love how in all the frenzy sometimes miracles happen. People smile when they hear children singing. They let go of differences and forgive the ones who've hurt them. And sometimes they even fall in love—like Mack and Kelley.

I was so thrilled to be asked to participate in this duet with Patricia Thayer, an author whose work I've admired for a long time. We had many interesting (and long!) phone calls between Nova Scotia and California! The experience was truly unforgettable.

I do hope you enjoy these tales of the Hughes sisters. And, from my house to yours, I wish you the merriest of Christmases.

Much love,

Donna

To Darrell…
you somehow know exactly when I need a push
and when I need a hug. This one's for you,
with love from Donna Alward.

CHAPTER ONE

KELLEY HUGHES SNAPPED the cell phone closed as her feet automatically stopped outside the gray brick building. She looked up at the burgundy-colored awning, furrowed her brow. Was it some sort of sign that she stopped, at just this moment, in front of Mack's Kitchen? Because she'd just assured her sister, Amelia, that she would have Christmas dinner under control, when the truth was she'd barely given it a thought.

She'd been so preoccupied thinking about Gram and the ranch that the holidays had crept up on her. She'd also realized lately that Amelia put on a brave face but she was handling a lot on her own. Kelley wanted to help. She thought now she should have volunteered some other service, because she simply didn't cook!

Surely there wasn't much to making a dinner. You put a turkey in the oven and cooked some vegetables, right? She bit down on her lip, staring at the green garland and twinkle lights decorating the iron railings. What had she been thinking? She hadn't even done her shopping yet and she was taking on something more? She looked at her watch; she should get back to the hospital. But there was the small matter of the nonexistent shopping she'd done. A display in the window caught her eye—a cookie-making kit, complete with cookie cutters and bright-red and green sprinkles. It was just the kind of thing Amelia would love to do with Jesse. Already she was mentally crossing the first gift off her list.

Then there would only be the gifts for Gram and Jesse, and

she could get back to the hospital. She didn't like leaving Gram alone for long, despite the older woman's insistence she'd be fine.

Gram kept her spirits up, but Kelley had seen fear in Gram's eyes for the first time she could remember. Yes, she would buy her gifts as quickly as possible and hurry back.

She opened the door, surprised by the old-fashioned bell above the door that announced her entrance. The next thing she noticed was the smell, and she paused. It smelled like every holiday rolled into one. Cinnamon and fruit and something else…baked bread? Her house never smelled like this. Ever. Carols played softly over invisible speakers, adding to the homey, holiday warmth.

This was Mack Dennison's latest store in his Mack's Kitchen franchise. After three years of building them from San Diego to Seattle, he'd finally come home to Montana and opened one himself. The Rebel Ridge weekly paper had done a feature on him just last week—the hometown boy who had made his fortune and brought it back to Helena. The sharp, savvy man in the picture hadn't jived with the vague memory she had of him from school. Now instead of the tiny house where he'd grown up in Rebel Ridge, he probably had some fancy condo here in the city. But there was no doubt that his stores were welcoming, homey, and stocked to the teeth with anything a cook could possibly want—and then some.

The walls and shelves were lined with pots, pans and unfathomable utensils with funny names. Another section heralded the latest in spices and gourmet combinations, specialty foods and recipe books. And smack dab in the middle was the counter and cash register, and a tall, good-looking man in jeans and a ribbed sweater. It suddenly dawned on her it was Mack. He was speaking to a middle-aged woman while bagging her items. She hadn't actually expected to see him here. After all, he was head of a successful chain of stores. She'd pictured him in a corporate tower somewhere. The smile she'd worn at the sound of a favorite carol faded away. If she'd known he'd be working the register…well, she might have reconsidered coming in.

When Mack smiled at his customer, Kelley's stomach did a

flip. It was a good smile, with an even row of teeth and a half dimple that popped in his cheek. He probably didn't even remember her. Somehow she'd always seemed to fade into the woodwork, and that was fine with her.

"Can I help you?"

She blinked, looked up and tried very hard to make her polite smile more relaxed. "Hello, Mack."

He hadn't changed much. A little older, but still with that tall, lean build, only slightly filled out now that he was past his teenage years. Dark eyes met hers, making something tingle down her spine. And his half-crooked smile was so infectious she smiled back. She couldn't help it.

"I'm sorry, have we met?"

Embarrassment flamed in her cheeks, and her smile faltered. Of course he wouldn't remember her now, if he hadn't even known she'd existed then. "You probably don't remember me. I'm Kelley Hughes. I was in your eleventh-grade math class."

His smile dimmed the slightest bit, and she wondered why, but just like that it was back up to its brilliant wattage and she wondered if it had actually happened at all.

"Of course. I remember now. Kelley Hughes. Your family runs the Rocking H." He held out his hand.

She was sure he was being polite. After a long pause, she held out her hand and let him shake it. The little flutters happened again, quite unexpectedly. He held it a little longer than she'd anticipated, and she pulled her fingers out of his.

"It's been a while," she said quietly. She put her hands in her pockets as she didn't know what else to do with them. Her ability to make small talk seemed to have fled, as well. She'd tried to leave high school behind for the most part, certainly shunning reunions and well-intentioned get togethers. She and Mack had never run in the same circles, anyway. She had been busy with the ranch after Grandpa died, and Mack had disappeared to build his empire, traveling the world. They might both be in Montana again now, but they were miles apart.

He shifted his weight at the long lull in conversation. "So…what are you up to these days? What brings you from Rebel Ridge into Helena?"

He was more adept at chitchat than she was, that much was clear. She chanced a look up into his eyes, and for a moment she was caught there. There was something…a tiny flash.

He put a hand on her arm, and she felt the warmth through her heavy jacket, none of the desire to pull away as she'd expected. But before she could think too much about it, he continued on. "I heard about your grandfather's passing. I'm so sorry. How is Mrs. Hughes?"

His inquiry surprised her. Small towns were just that, and in a place like Rebel Ridge everyone tended to ask after everyone else's family. She was sure he was just being polite again. But the concern touched her nevertheless. Especially now.

Her throat thickened with the emotion she'd held in all day.

She moved away, under the pretext of examining the wares on the shelves nearby. It wasn't that she didn't love the ranch; she did. And right now it was more important to her than ever. But in the back of her mind there was something else that she couldn't shake—there'd never been a question on her part, never been an opportunity to do anything else. She'd worked hard, had looked after things. But there had been places she'd wanted to see, things she'd wanted to do. Mack had left Rebel Ridge behind and had gone on to build his own business. He'd had a choice.

But responsibility weighed even more heavily on her these days. The whole trip to Helena was for Gram's angioplasty at the hospital, and it was a stark reminder that things were changing.

"Gram's doing fine." She felt a slight twinge at glossing over the truth, but what did it matter? It wasn't as if she'd see Mack again. She rarely came into town. She was only here for the week because they hadn't wanted to leave Gram on her own. And Mack was busy, now that he'd become somewhat of a local celebrity. She was sure his life here in Helena was busier than it had ever been when they'd both lived in "the Ridge." She was only here to shop.

A pause settled over the pair once more. As the silence drew out, she tried to ignore the way his jeans hugged his body, the breadth of his shoulders or the fluttering that kept happening in her tummy. It was unfamiliar and she didn't like it. The glimmer of attraction was as foreign to her as the merchandise he carried.

Kelley pasted on another smile for the sake of manners. "I really came in to find a Christmas present for my sister."

Mack's shoulders relaxed. "What did you have in mind?"

"I saw that cookie kit in the window. I'm sure she'd enjoy doing something like that with her son."

He went to a shelf and pulled out one of the kits she'd seen. Cookies cutters in the shapes of snowflakes, trees and snowmen danced beneath the plastic coating. Sprinkles and gumdrops were in tiny packages for decorating.

It was exactly the sort of thing Amelia would love. Kelley could give it to her early, and Amelia and Jesse would mix up dough and have a wonderful time cutting out shapes and decorating them for the holidays. The thought put a little ache in her chest. Jesse was such a blessing and a bright spot in their lives.

Kelley reached out and took the kit from Mack's hands, running a finger down the jar of red crystalized sugar. Amelia was a wonderful mom, but Jesse wanted a dad. He'd started school this year and was suddenly noticing things were different in his friends' homes. And he'd whispered to Kelley the other day that he'd wished for a dad for Christmas. It had touched her, made her wistful. She let him help out on the ranch, showed him things. But she was Aunt Kelley, not a father. It wasn't anywhere near the same.

"It's perfect," she murmured. "Amelia and Jesse will have a wonderful time." Jesse was so worried about his great-grandmother. Maybe this would help fill in the gaps that couldn't truly be filled. Gaps that she herself had been noticing more lately, in herself. Resentments that bubbled up from nowhere. Longings—the female kind—that had no place in the foreman of a ranch. A need to be more than that somehow. And not knowing how—or if—she should begin.

But there was no time for those thoughts now. She had her hands full with the Rocking H and looking after Amelia and

Ruby. It had always been that way and wasn't likely to change anytime soon.

She looked up at him, unprepared for the expression mirrored back at her.

His dark eyes were soft with what might have been understanding, his lips unsmiling. "Yes," he said quietly. "Kids like baking and decorating. And Mrs. Hughes, too, I expect."

"She probably won't be up to it after—"

Kelley broke off, realizing that she'd said too much as his brows pulled together.

"After what?" The spell that had been tenuously woven around them dissipated. She averted her eyes.

"Nothing."

But he'd already picked up on the hesitation in her voice. "Is there something wrong? You did say she was fine. But you sound upset."

"She is…she will be. It's nothing."

And yet it was. Somehow talking in riddles to Mack brought emotions to the surface, and she swallowed, trying to beat them back. Gram was the glue. She and Grandpa had raised them after the deaths of their parents, and then Gram had kept the ranch going after Grandpa's death several years ago. Kelley had stepped in as she'd always known she eventually would, but it was Gram that was the heart and soul of the Hughes clan, and her illness made Kelley suddenly realize there might not be that many more Christmases with them all together. She blinked and picked up a package that read Chili Pickled Pears. The label blurred.

"Kelley."

She looked up in alarm. The way he said her name sounded somewhere between a command and an endearment. It was silly considering she hadn't seen him for nearly a decade. He'd been busy making his way in the world and she'd stayed in exactly the same place where they'd grown up. But in his eyes was a gentle invitation and she found herself revealing more than she'd planned.

"I'm in Helena because Gram's in the hospital," she explained, her throat tightening once more.

"Is it serious?"

"She's had some tests, and she's scheduled for an angio-plasty tomorrow."

Mack placed a hand on her arm and she felt the warmth soak through her jacket and sleeve, right to her skin. Rather than re-pelling, it was comforting. "I hadn't heard."

"It isn't exactly community knowledge. She wanted to keep it quiet. The doctors say she'll be fine, but…"

"It's a bit scary," he finished.

"Yes," she admitted. She hadn't spoken to anyone of her fears about Gram. Mack was the very first person who seemed to care about how *she* might be feeling, and for that reason alone, she found herself responding to his gentle comments.

For some strange reason she thought it might be nice to be comforted in his arms. But that was insane. She didn't do physical touches. And she wasn't sure she'd know how to accept comfort, anyway. Her own two feet was how she normally dealt with things. She didn't rely on other people. Perhaps that was why the thought of losing Gram panicked her so much. Gram was the one person Kelley had *always* counted on.

She cleared her throat. "Anyway," she continued, "with my nephew Jesse in school, Amelia couldn't really come, and we didn't want to leave Gram here alone. So I'm staying at a motel near the hospital until it's over and I can take her home."

"I'm sorry, Kelley. This must be difficult, especially so close to the holidays." His fingers squeezed, reassuring. "If there's anything I can do to help…everyone in Rebel Ridge knows and loves Mrs. Hughes."

Yes, everyone loved Ruby. And Amelia. If Kelley didn't hold the family together, who would? But then, what was left for her? It was a heavy load, trying to be all things for all people.

The afternoon was waning and she still had to pick up other gifts. "I should get going," she said, hiding a sigh and taking her purchase up to the cash register. "I need to finish up my shopping and get back to the hospital. And the forecast said there's a storm coming."

"When did you eat last, Kelley?"

She met his gaze, a bit confused at his concern. "Me? Why?"

"Because you look a little pale. And like you could use a bite. Here, try this." He plucked a small square from a silver tray and held it in front of her mouth.

She looked at his hand warily, holding out some sort of sweet. It smelled wonderful, spicy and rich. She swallowed, but her mouth watered, anyway, and her tummy rumbled the slightest bit. She shifted her gaze to his face and he raised one eyebrow.

She opened her mouth, and he popped the morsel into it.

Mmmm. Chewy, moist, rich and spicy. She closed her eyes. Just this one bite was far better than anything she'd had at the hospital cafeteria today. Or any day this week, since that was where she'd had most of her meals.

"What *is* that?"

With a self-satisfied smile, he picked up her package of pickled pears. "Fruitcake."

But she hated fruitcake. Normally.

"Try what's on the other tray."

She reached over and picked up an odd-looking packet, golden brown. The cube of fruitcake had only increased her hunger and she took a substantial bite. Flavor exploded on her tongue…pastry and butter and…was that ham? Something tasted like dill. She ate the rest without hesitation. "That's really good, Mack." The compliment didn't hurt as much as she'd expected it would. She offered her first, unfettered, genuine smile. "Not bad for a boy from the Ridge."

"I can share the recipe if you like."

Once again she felt awkward and her smile wavered. She was no domestic goddess and most of the time felt no need to apologize for it. But lately she'd had stirrings…a vague sense of dissatisfaction that while she was great at running the ranch, as a woman she was a bit of a failure. And then a resulting anger at herself because in her heart she knew that not being able to cook and sew and do all those things Amelia was a natural at didn't make her less of a woman.

No, the reasons went far deeper than that, in scars that would never go away.

"I could take it for Amelia." She didn't want to admit she couldn't even make boxed macaroni and cheese. "I'm in charge of the ranch. Amelia runs the house." She smiled politely. "We play to our strengths." The fact that her sister was the nurturer of all of them, including being a fantastic single parent, made Kelley proud.

"So you don't cook…at all?"

The surprised tone of his voice took any shred of femininity she'd had and threw it out the window. She was suddenly aware of what she was wearing—faded jeans and a serviceable, sexless jacket. Even her scarf now seemed a dull shade of brown. Grandpa had often teased that she was his "boy," and at one time it had made her proud. But then she'd had glimpses of her own dreams, which were brought to a sharp end when he was gone and it was up to her to keep things going for Amelia and Grandma Ruby. Lord knew Ruby was still the head of the family, but she wasn't up to the task of the physical running of the ranch. That was left to Kelley. She'd known her duty and had done it.

But his surprise at her lack of culinary skills made her bristle. "Actually, I'm cooking the family Christmas dinner this year." Up went her chin again. She'd be damned if she'd let him know that the extent of her cooking was frying a plain old egg for breakfast or putting together a sandwich. She grew suddenly inspired. "As a matter of fact, while I'm here I can look for some new and interesting ideas to add to the meal."

New and interesting indeed. She knew nothing about putting on a dinner, but she was sure she could do it. She'd never failed at anything she'd tried before. It only took diligence and hard work, like any other difficult task.

"Oh, that's a shame, then. I was thinking you should come take a class. I run them through the week, for all sorts of people. Men and women, young and old. We start with boiling water. It's a bird course—impossible to fail. But if you're interested in ideas…"

A cooking school? She hadn't taken home ec the first time, and she sure didn't want to do it now. Besides, remembering high school was a huge source of pain for her. She'd rather just leave it all behind. She probably wouldn't even have come in today if she'd known he was going to be here. "I don't have the time for anything elaborate."

She set her teeth. Just because she didn't cook didn't mean she couldn't. She could still hear the skepticism in Amelia's voice when she'd offered to do the dinner on Christmas Day. Her laugh had been followed by the suggestion of a caterer. It had been good-natured sisterly teasing, but it had stung just the same. Now, looking up in Mack's handsome face, she really felt as though she had something to prove.

"Would what I tasted work as an appetizer? For my Christmas dinner? You did say you had the recipe."

Briefly she imagined bringing out a tray with warm, golden-brown parcels, serving perhaps a glass of wine or punch before dinner while Jesse played with his new toys and carols played on the stereo. What would Amelia say then? Amelia had been so determined to look after the ranch work in Kelley's absence. Surely Kelley could prove herself equally adept at Amelia's forte. She was getting so tired of being the sister in jeans and boots. There was more to her than that. Maybe she was finally ready to let someone see it.

"Absolutely. They're easy as anything."

She highly doubted it, but they couldn't be that hard could they? "That would be great, Mack. I appreciate it."

He jotted down the recipe on a card and put it in the bag with the rest of her purchases. "You'll need some of my dill seasoning. The rest of the items you can buy at the grocery store."

He put in a bottle and rang in the pears and cookie kit. At the last moment he took a small bag from beneath the counter and tucked it in with her purchases.

"A little treat for Ruby, if you can sneak it in."

"I'll do that." She paid and put the receipt in her wallet.

"Give my best to your family, Kelley."

"I will."

She was nearly to the door, tugging her mittens back over her hands, when she heard his warm voice once more, sending a delicious shiver down her arms.

"And, Kelley?"

She half turned to look back at him.

"Merry Christmas."

For some inexplicable reason, the simple wish made the backs of her eyes sting. She pulled on her mitten, gripped the door handle and stepped out into the bitter cold.

CHAPTER TWO

"DAMMIT!"

Kelley dropped the pan onto the stovetop, fanning away smoke as she sucked on her burned finger.

The puffs were ruined, completely ruined. She took off the oven mitt and went to the window, pushing it open a crack and letting the cold air in and the acrid smell out. She'd picked up the rest of the ingredients on Mack's list and taken them back to the motel thinking a trial run would help her pass the time while the storm blew outside.

Only, there'd been a flaw in her plan. The one aluminum baking sheet in the kitchenette cupboard now appeared charred beyond repair. The tops of the phyllo puffs were burned. And several of the pastry sheets lay shredded on the small counter-top amid a mess of prosciutto, parmesan, asparagus and Mack's dill seasoning. The mess was held together by bits of greasy melted butter that hadn't behaved...perhaps because she hadn't had something the recipe called a pastry brush. She'd tried using the curved end of a fork, but it had made nothing but a mess.

She was in deep, deep trouble. She pushed back a few strands of hair that had escaped her braid. The recipe had sounded simple. If she couldn't even make a simple hors d'oeuvre, how could she expect to pull off a whole dinner without burning down the house?

A knock sounded on the motel door as she dumped the whole lot of ruined food in the garbage. "Hello? Everyone okay in there?"

And the pan froze in her hand.

Okay, so she was thinking about Mack, and the way he'd held her hand longer than necessary today. That was the only reason it sounded like his voice outside.

She went to the door and looked out the peep hole.

"Oh, no," she breathed, pressing her hands to her cheeks and attempting to smooth her wild hair. She looked a fright. It *was* Mack. His dark eyes were flashing, his jaw taut as he lifted his hand to bang on the door again. She jumped at the harsh contact of fist to wood, her heart taking up a frantic hammering.

"Are you okay? I can smell smoke!" She heard the urgent tone of his voice and had the desperate thought he'd do something stupid like call 911 if she didn't answer.

"Hello? Answer me!"

Oh, hell! What if he broke down the door?

"Just a minute," she called, spinning in a frantic circle.

She opened the door, stood firmly in the breach. Snow swirled around Mack's head as his shoulders hunched against the storm.

"Kelley?"

Busted. "What in the world are you doing here?" she demanded, attempting to look defiant though her pulse was still pounding.

"I could smell smoke and was afraid of a fire." Without a how do you do, he pushed by her and into the room. "Is everything okay?"

"Perfectly fine."

She hated how the words came out with a quaver at the end, or how his bursting past her sent a spiral of fear from her head to the tip of her toes. Alone, in a motel room, with a man she didn't exactly know. Memories rushed back, sharp as knives, and she beat them aside angrily. She was sick to death of them having power over her.

"Is that awful smell asparagus puffs?"

Humiliation made her want to sink through the floor, and she had the thought that at least it would provide an escape route. She instinctively shuffled sideways so that she had the door directly behind her. "It was. Definitely past tense."

He coughed. "What did you cook them with, a blow torch? At least I know you're all right and not setting the entire motel on fire."

His obvious concern alleviated a bit of panic she'd inevitably felt at his bursting in. "What in the world are you doing here?"

He shook his head, sending snowflakes sprinkling off his hair. "I'm staying next door. Until my house is finished."

"Your house?" What was he talking about? He was living here? And building a house?

"You didn't know?"

She shook her head. "No."

"I thought the people in Rebel Ridge kept the grapevine going better. Mabel Reese must be slacking. I'm building a house out on the bluff."

She refused to be charmed by his reference to the town gossip who kept everyone in the know whether they wanted to be or not. "And you're here…" She went to close the window and left the idea hanging, still aware that if it came to it, she could reach the doorway first.

He smiled, popping the one dimple most unfairly. "You mentioned a motel in the shop today. I had no idea it was this one. Small world, huh?"

Too small to her mind.

He wrinkled his nose, raked his gaze over her dough-studded clothing and said, "Oh, boy."

And then it suddenly dawned on her that here stood a man who was capable of helping her with her problem. Just not tonight. Not in a motel room. Her blood momentarily seemed to run cold. If she could just ask him, and get rid of him, it would be fine. If he agreed, they'd meet somewhere she felt safe. A controlled environment, like his cooking school. One with lots of people around.

Mack looked around him at the mess everywhere. The bed was the only untouched area in the room. Kelley Hughes, class wallflower, stood before him in old jeans spotted with what looked like dough and spots of grease. Her hair was coming out of her braid and her cheeks were flushed. She had a hard time meeting his eyes.

Everything about her made his blood leap. She was beautiful this way, less than perfect, without the cool control she had exhibited this afternoon. Though he could tell she was trying hard. He hadn't remembered her at first, not until she'd said her name and he remembered the quiet girl who'd sat at the back of his math class. She'd been the studious type, and he'd been too withdrawn to say anything to her anyway.

The acrid smell was horrible, but his nose detected what was likely pastry and ham. He hid a smile. He'd been correct on the first guess…asparagus puffs. Nothing was burning down. It was just burned.

Her soft voice interrupted his analysis. "I'm afraid the puffs didn't turn out as I expected."

"What happened?"

She looked as if she was about to swallow a canary. Despite her words this afternoon, he'd bet his boots she couldn't cook. Someone who could wouldn't have looked so uncomfortable surrounded by pots and utensils.

She took a deep breath. "I can't cook. Not a bit."

"No kidding." A grin tugged the corner of his mouth as her eyes narrowed.

"Look, save the smart remarks, okay? I promised everyone a Christmas Day dinner…I can't ask my sister to put more on her plate. She's looking after the ranch right now while I'm gone, and there's her son, Jesse, and she's going to have Gram when she comes home—" She broke off, took a breath. "But you have a cooking school. You could help."

Well, well. She was asking for help after all. It surprised him.

"Yes, lessons are once a week, above the store."

Snow melted off his dark hair, trickling in a cold path down the back of his neck. He saw the glimmer of despair in her eyes. His regular cooking classes wouldn't cut it, not with the tight timing, and they both knew it. "But Christmas is in days, not weeks," he added.

"I'm aware of that." She sighed. But there was something else behind it, and he wasn't sure what. She looked, at this moment, as if she'd like to be somewhere else. Anywhere else.

"Do you want *me* to cook dinner for your family?"

It was only dinner. Surely it didn't matter that much *who* cooked it. What mattered was being together, or so he was told.

Kelley folded her hands in front of her, and he saw the red tip on her index finger—she'd burned herself.

"That would be the easy way, I suppose. But, no, thank you. I need to do this myself."

She jutted her chin. "Right now you're the only one I can think of to help me. I want you to show me, Mack. I need to do this. I need to prove to them I can do it." She turned her hazel eyes up to him. "I need to prove it to myself."

He swallowed against the rush of something he didn't want to acknowledge. Someone needed him. And that was a rarity.

"Will you teach me how to make a Christmas dinner for my family?"

Mack fought back the sudden urge to hug her. The woman standing before him now thought she looked tough, he was sure of it. She obviously cared deeply about her family—that scored points with him.

Her imploring eyes were exactly the sort of reason he'd started Mack's Kitchen in the first place. And maybe helping her would make Christmas something to look forward to this year, take away the monotony of the holiday. Help him to forget why he'd never bought in to the whole Christmas magic thing. The one time he had…it had been a disaster.

Holiday cheer wasn't for him, but he understood other people's need for it. "I'll help you."

"You will?"

He chuckled at the astonishment he heard in her voice. "Yes, I will. Teaching is what I do, and from what you've said, no one else in your family is up to it. Besides—" he looked around him at the mess, slid his gaze back to hers "—I do enjoy a challenge."

"Ha-ha."

"And since I can't see us making it out to buy any groceries right now, how much phyllo have you got left? We might as well get started."

"Here?" Kelley's eyes darted from him to the door and back, her jumbled-up nerves suddenly back with a vengeance. She'd meant at his *store*. At his place of business. Not a motel room in the middle of the night! "I don't think that's a good idea."

"Are you expecting someone?" he asked.

The worldly question sent a blush straight up her neck. "No! Of course not!" Her eyes widened further as his dimple flashed again and she realized he was teasing. There wasn't much time before Christmas and she had a lot of work to do. But a motel room?

"Come on, this is much more fun than being stuck with only the television for company. Besides, you fall off the horse, you get right back on. It can't be that bad."

She followed him into the kitchen and realized how it must look to him. It was a complete disaster.

He grinned and that damnable dimple flashed again. "Okay, so I was wrong. It *can* be that bad." A laugh rippled out of his throat. "Sit tight. I'm going to pop back next door for a minute." He got to the door and looked back. "And Kelley? Don't touch *anything*."

Moments later he was back carrying his own kitchenette-stocked cookie sheet, a half head of broccoli, a box of eggs, cheese and a tiny spice bottle.

"What's all that?"

"Dinner."

Kelley hadn't followed his instructions to the letter, but she'd cleaned a tidy space on the counter. He put the sheet on the stovetop and rubbed his hands together. "Okay," he said. "First the pastry."

Kelley stood several feet away as he went to get the phyllo. He had no idea how uncomfortable she was right now, and she'd cut off her own arm before she'd explain. In her head she knew the quiet boy she remembered was harmless. But her subconscious kept shouting something else. She wasn't used to being railroaded, and he'd burst in tonight and taken over. But she was the foreman of a ranch. She could do this.

"Kelley, you can't cook from over there." He beckoned her over. She swallowed and quietly went to his side. Gently he showed her how to separate the sheets and lay them out carefully. "Where's your pastry brush?"

"I haven't got one."

He muttered an exclamation and picked up the bowl of melted butter. "That's why it looks so torn, then. We'll have to improvise."

He turned his head to look at her and she shrugged. "Improvise?"

He laughed at her simple response. "You know."

She still didn't get his meaning. Improvise what?

"Okay, so you don't know. Let's put it in ranch terms. Imagine there's a fence line broken and you left your tools somewhere. What do you do?"

"You're going to equate pastry with fences." The analogy relaxed her in spite of herself and she leaned forward, watching the motion of his hands.

"Don't be so narrow-minded. Look. We use our fingers instead. Come here. Dip and spread." She put her hands on the dough, and he quickly reached out to stop her. "Gently," he said quietly, holding her hand in his and guiding it, smoothing the butter on the phyllo.

Kelley's stomach clenched, full of nerves. His hands were firm and sure on hers, the slick texture of the butter warm beneath their fingertips as they smoothed it over the fragile sheets. His body nestled close behind her; she could feel the strong heat of it against her back as he guided her hands. Never in the last decade had she let a man get this close to her. There'd never been a need at Rocking H for personal contact.

She was sure he couldn't tell the battle waging within her—the thin, sharp thread of fear warring with a shocking need to feel close to him. Or her surprise at realizing she *wanted* to feel close to him. This afternoon his quiet concern had been genuine, and something told her that she was safe.

She chanced a look up at him. Big mistake. For in the moment she turned her head to look up, he looked down, and their gazes caught. His pupils were dark. Not teasing at all, but open and curious, like he was trying to see right down into the core of her. She hadn't expected this at all...not Mack, not cooking, and certainly not the knot of awareness that was settling low within her.

There was something here. She caught her lip between her teeth and worried it. Right now they had their hands in butter and all she could think was how good-looking he was, the way he had tiny crinkles at the corners of his eyes or how broad his shoulders were as she was snuggled between them.

She bit down on her lip, fighting back the instinctive fear that rose up without warning.

"What's next?" She made herself say something to break the silence.

A slow smile formed on his lips and Kelley felt completely out of her depth. She hadn't meant it as an innuendo of any sort, but what else would he think as she stood there staring at him like a lovesick kitten? She had to stop this. She wasn't interested in Mack Dennison, or *any* man for that matter. What she wanted was to bake prosciutto and asparagus puffs.

She held his gaze but stiffened her shoulders. "I meant with the recipe."

To her amazement the smile grew bigger. "I assumed nothing less."

Kelley huffed and turned away. That was enough of being silly and making calf eyes. "You've certainly broken out of your shy shell."

"You can't build a business by hiding away in a closet."

She wanted to reach out and give him a push, but then remembered that her fingers were coated in butter. She moved away to the sink where she rinsed and dried her hands, away from his body, feeling safer with distance. "Are you saying you had to force yourself?"

"That's exactly what I'm saying. I don't know if you noticed, but I wasn't the most personable kid in class. I had to learn to meet people. To like people. So I did."

She wished she could shed her old self so easily. She turned away. "I thought you were going to help."

"And so I am. Just having a little fun. Don't you think this should be fun?"

Kelley remembered holding Gram's hand as she lay in the cardiac care unit. And little Jesse's face as he whispered to her what he'd asked for for Christmas. All the little resentments faded away in those moments; family was everything. She squared her shoulders.

"I need to do this, Mack, and cooking is beyond me."

"Okay."

She paused, surprised at his easy acceptance. "That's it?" He wasn't going to bait her more or tease her or ask her why it was so difficult?

"Don't be so hard on yourself. You run a ranch, for Pete's sake. You can't be expected to do everything well."

"I'm not used to being incapable."

"And I bet it kills you to admit it." He grinned.

She raised an eyebrow and he relented. He touched her again, his hand resting on her shoulder. He'd touched her more today than any man had in a long time. What was odd was that it wasn't accompanied by her usual instinct to run or curl into a ball.

"All teasing aside. Everyone can cook, once they learn how. You've just never learned, that's all." He stepped back and reached for some of the thinly sliced ham. "Then let's cook, Kelley. I promise you, it won't be all that painful."

When she looked at his warm smile, she knew he was wrong. Because already she was feeling a tightness around her chest that had little to do with cooking.

Together they layered on ham, asparagus, fresh parmesan and Mack's dill seasoning. He showed her how to fold the pastry over and slice it, laying each piece on his own baking tray. He slid it into the oven and showed her how to work the timer…all without making her feel stupid or inept. All with little touches, correcting her hand or showing her how to slice the rounds without tearing. Touches that she sensed meant nothing to him. And maybe that was why she seemed to accept them. He was in his role of teacher.

When it was done he found a larger mixing bowl. Kelley stared as he put it on the counter and stepped back. "Now what are you doing?"

"I'm not. You are. You're going to make us dinner. A few appetizers does not a meal make."

"But I can't…"

He merely raised an eyebrow. "You can. This was one of the first things we learned to make in home ec. Mrs. Farber was a strict one, remember her?"

Kelley turned a pot holder over in her fingers. "I never took home ec, remember?"

"Oh, right." He seemed oblivious to her discomfort and continued on. "She had this saying…a place for everything and everything in its place. She was terrifying. But she knew how to cook and she knew how to teach it. So tonight I get to pass the torch."

She angled him a dry look.

"Right, well, maybe no torches."

She couldn't help the smile that trembled on her lips at his joke. "What am I making?"

"Crustless quiche."

She couldn't help it; she rolled her eyes. "Quiche? Seriously?"

"You can scramble the eggs if you want, but this is much better and hardly more work. We don't have proper pastry, so we'll go crustless."

A small search revealed one round baking dish. In no time Kelley had whipped eggs, grated cheese, added in bits of broccoli and some of the leftover ham from the asparagus rolls and a dash of something from a bottle Mack had brought with him. It all poured into the buttered pan, ready to go in the oven the moment the appetizers came out.

"I did that."

"Yep." He leaned back against the counter with a satisfied smile as she slid the oven mitt off her hand. The perfectly browned puffs were on the stove, cooling.

"I have a quiche in the oven."

"Indeed. Usually we don't get to that until lesson two, but you did a great job."

Kelley looked up at him. He'd been a gentleman. He'd been patient and understanding and easy to be around.

"Thank you, Mack."

She didn't know how to put the rest into words without sounding encouraging, so she simply let herself smile, and popped one of the fresh bites in her mouth. Delicious. And not a burn mark on them.

"I forgot. I brought one more thing."

Mack boosted himself away from the counter and went to the fridge. He took out a bottle of white wine and a Swiss Army knife from his pocket. Within seconds he'd flipped out a corkscrew.

Kelley got two glasses from the cupboard. She could hardly kick him out after he'd helped her…and provided most of the groceries. The hour they'd spent cooking had gone a long way in gaining a simple, yet tentative trust.

"Tumblers?"

She laughed. "What do I look like, the Waterford factory?"

"They'll do, then. Though to be fair…this is more of a whiskey joint sort of place."

He poured the wine into the glasses as lovely smells came out of the oven. Kelley grabbed a plate and put the asparagus rolls on it, moving to the tiny drop-leaf table that was set up in the outer area of the motel room.

"This wasn't the dinner you planned tonight, I bet."

"No."

"How's your grandmother?"

His asking pleased her. "Hanging in there. Her procedure has been postponed, though." She was surprised but touched by the concern in his eyes. "Not because of her condition," she added hastily. "The weather warning. The hospital is postponing nonemergency procedures until after the storm."

"And she's going to be fine?"

"The doctor says so. But…"

She stopped as a lump formed in her throat. Grandma Ruby was everything to her and Amelia. She took a sip of wine, unwilling to put voice to her fears.

At her long silence, Mack leaned forward. "Is it worse than you said? Is there more? What's the *but?*"

"But she has a heart condition, and it has really made us realize that she's getting older. That she won't be around forever. And so maybe part of this whole Christmas thing is just me wondering how many more Christmases we'll all have together. I don't know what I'd do without her, Mack."

It was an intimate confession, especially between the two

of them; two people that had always known *of* each other but had never been friends. She didn't know why she was able to talk to him so easily. Maybe because in many ways he was a stranger, and it was easier to admit things when there was that bit of natural distance between them.

Mack reached across the small table and took her hand in his. All she could do was squeeze back.

Kelley stared down at their joined fingers. Mack's thumb rubbed over the top of her hand, the friction creating a warmth she was unused to. Normally she would have pulled away immediately. But this time she accepted the simple touch.

"I'm sure she's going to be fine. Try not to worry so much."

Kelley pulled her hand away. "I'm just out of sorts. I'm not used to being away from the ranch for so long, the main phone lines are down, and Amelia's not answering her cell phone. She probably forgot to charge it."

"I take it that's happened before."

A smile flirted with the edges of her lips. "A time or two. But the reception at the house isn't always the best, either."

"So why didn't she bring Ruby into town?"

Kelley took a sip of the wine. She licked the remnants off her lips and sighed. "It's harder for her. She has Jesse to worry about now, and he's started school. You've seen my cooking." This got a smile. "We'd all starve if it were left to me. I hired an extra hand to help out while I was gone, but I don't know if he arrived before the storm or not. Amelia insisted she could manage. But I just don't know."

"You really don't have much faith in people, do you?"

The quiet question unsettled her. Maybe what had happened to her made her lose faith. She kept to her inner circle—her family—and today's foray into the cooking world with Mack was definitely an aberration. The ding of the oven timer saved her from answering.

She went to take the quiche out while Mack went to the window and parted the curtains, looking out. "It's picked up out there. You can't even see across the street."

Kelley looked over at him, feeling the intimacy grow, unsure what to do about it. Here they were, shut up in a small motel room in the middle of the first real storm of the year. She pushed away the nervousness that suddenly popped up again. She didn't do well in closed spaces. At least the lights were on. "Good thing you're just next door. It's a short commute."

He laughed, the sound warm and masculine. "You wouldn't send me away before dinner, would you?"

She suddenly wanted him to go, but somehow wanted him to stay, too. The thought of being here alone in the blizzard seemed so dismal that she nearly welcomed the company. Normally when a storm was coming, she bunked up at the house with Gram and Amelia and Jesse. Amelia looked after everyone and Kelley played board games with her nephew. Being stuck in town at a half-rate motel wasn't quite as heart-warming. Somehow having Mack with her made her feel safer, and that was unexpected.

"You helped me make it. I suppose it's unlikely you'll be poisoned."

Again the laugh...my word, he laughed easily, and it sent ripples of pleasure down her arms. Kelley reached up for plates in the tiny cupboard, ignoring the quiver in her belly that his voice ignited. She handed him a plate, but he paused with it between their hands.

"Would you *like* me to be poisoned?"

She looked up into his eyes, bright with teasing. He was having fun with her. And she liked it. The moment held. Her breath caught as his smile faded and his gaze dropped to her open lips.

Was he considering kissing her?

Breath came back in with a rush of panic on its heels as she thrust the plate in his hand. "Keep it up and I'll find a way."

He reached into a drawer and pulled out a knife for cutting the quiche. He put it into her hand, his fingers warm over hers as she gripped the handle. He was a touchy one! She shivered as he leaned close to her ear and whispered, "Poison's cleaner, but a knife will do the trick in a pinch."

That was it. She stomped her foot and wheeled. "Stop it, you infernal tease!"

The lights flickered. They looked up at the fixture together, and then everything went dark.

CHAPTER THREE

"Power's out."

"Thanks, Einstein." She put the knife back on the counter next to the warm quiche and tried to cover her sudden unease. His form was dark, his face shadowed in the dimness. The intimacy of earlier was back, sharp and immediate. She tried to make her heart stop pounding so furiously, make her breaths regular. She put several feet of countertop between them.

Mack was already searching the end table beside the bed for matches, and she watched his shadowed form with her heart in her throat. She tried to push the memories away. He was not Wilcox, and this was not an abandoned cabin in the middle of nowhere.

This was Mack, in a motel room; in the dark; in the middle of the first big blizzard of the year. Her heart pounded against her ribs painfully.

"Any luck with matches?" he asked.

She jumped at the sound of his voice. "Not yet," she croaked, opening a single drawer with shaking fingers. A part of her wanted to reach out and let him shelter her. And yet the thought also scared her to death. She didn't know him well enough. His caring had drawn her to him tonight, but how well did she really know him? She didn't.

"Do you have a flashlight anywhere?"

His voice sounded huskier in the darkness and she swallowed thickly. "I think there's one in the truck. I can go look."

"In this weather?

"But we can't just sit here in the dark!"

She could tell he was grinning, even though she couldn't make out the details of his face.

"Why not? I do some of my best work in the dark."

"Stop smiling. This isn't funny." Indeed it was not. She was torn between fear of being alone and fear of being with him, and she was becoming more tied up in knots by the moment.

"Okay," he relented. "Look, the meal is cooked." He moved to stand beside her and picked up the knife. "Can you see enough to get some forks? We might as well eat while it's warm."

She nodded, but he caught her hesitancy. "Are you scared of the dark, Kelley?"

A tiny thread of hysteria bubbled inside her. The dark? That and then some. "A little."

"I used to be, too. I was hoping if I made light of it… But it didn't work, did it?" He reached out and kneaded her shoulders and she closed her eyes, focusing on the reassuring sound of his voice and not the horrible memories she kept trying to push away.

"How did you stop?" There was no sound in the room beyond their breathing. And then she held her breath and there was just him.

"I don't know. I guess I just stood up to it." His fingers rubbed the tendons on the side of her neck and she exhaled slowly. "It's okay. You're not alone in here. We've got shelter from the storm and we've even got dinner. You don't need to be afraid."

But she was afraid. "The walls feel small," she whispered, and to her surprise, he rested his chin on the top of her head.

"I know," he said, and her heart squeezed.

He gave her shoulders a final rub and backed away. "Let's have something to eat. Maybe after that the power will be back on."

She found utensils with shaky hands, and Mack scooped up servings for both of them. He was taking the plates to the table when a knock sounded at the door, the sharp sound making her jump yet again in the darkness.

"Hello? Miss Hughes?"

Kelley stood and went closer to the door. "Yes?"

"It's Jerry Smith, the owner. I wanted to make sure you're all right."

"I'm fine, thank you," she called through the door, and stepped forward to open it.

"Don't bother opening the door, miss, keep your heat in. There should be an emergency candle in the very bottom drawer beside the stove. Hopefully the power won't be out for long."

"Jerry," Mack called out, "it's Mack. No need to check on me."

Kelley blushed. Smith didn't know her, but Mack was a bit of a celebrity, and here they were in a motel room together. Her cheeks felt like fire and she pressed her cool fingers to them.

"Okay, Mack. I'll carry on. Colder 'n hell out here."

"You know the owner?" Kelley whispered.

"I've been here for two months already, remember?"

The chill was already seeping through the walls. "Come on," she suggested. "Let's eat before it gets cold."

Mack found the candle and a simple holder, put it in the middle of the tiny table and poured more wine. She sat stiffly and picked up her fork, ignoring the way the candlelight highlighted his cheekbones, throwing the hollows into shadow. "Let's just eat, and maybe by the time we're done, the lights will be back on." She let out a shaky breath. "I guess Jesse will get his white Christmas after all."

She took a bite of the quiche, surprised at how good it tasted. "It's not bad!"

"I told you anyone can cook." He took a bite of his own.

The candlelight flickered and she lifted her eyes to meet his. "It's not turkey and trimmings."

"We'll get you there," he smiled, and she smiled back.

For several minutes they made small talk about Rocking H and how he'd spent his time since high school seeking his fortune. The candle burned lower and the conversation grew lazy. She talked about Ruby and Amelia and mentioned Jesse's Christmas wish for a father and how it had touched her. The smile faded from his lips and his eyes grew serious.

"So if you could have one Christmas wish, what would it be?"

She opened her mouth to answer but he stopped her, holding up a finger. "Wait. One wish for Kelley. Not for anyone else."

What would she wish for? She had the ranch and Amelia and Gram and Jesse, and she loved them. But lately she had wondered what else was out there, for her. She'd always wanted to travel, see some of the world, meet new people and experience new things. Instead she'd been tied to the Rocking H in so many ways. And Mack had just told her how he'd gone and done all those things and had come back, successful, even rich. It made her wish seem foolish.

"More," she whispered finally. "I want more." She suddenly felt unbearably guilty for saying it, knowing she should be thankful for having so much. She pushed out her chair and went to the sink, holding on to the edge.

She heard Mack's chair scrape away from the tiny table. He stepped forward until he was only a breath away. Close enough she could smell him—soap and some sort of manly aftershave, somehow magnified in the semidarkness.

"Kelley, look at me."

"This is highly unusual." She spoke to the wall behind the sink. "We hardly know each other. I can't imagine why I've said as much as I have. I don't usually..." But she stopped. "Maybe this dinner isn't a good idea. I can have it catered—" she started to babble "—it really doesn't matter. And I need to get back as soon as possible..."

"Stop." Strong hands gripped her arms and turned her around. "Lord, it was a simple question."

She froze at the feeling of his hands on her arms. After a few seconds his fingers relaxed and she let out the breath she'd pulled in. Nothing about this evening was simple. Especially not the way he seemed able to knock down fences she'd erected years ago.

"Kelley," he murmured.

She felt like weeping. She'd tried to hide things tonight but apparently she'd failed. He'd seen clear through her bravado and attempt at coolness. She stared at his chest, focusing on a pewter medal that hung from a chain. "I want to see new places. I want to do things." In the darkness she seemed able to whisper her thoughts like a confession. "I want people to see me as more than the ranch foreman in dusty jeans and dirty boots."

She couldn't look at him, not when she was feeling this selfish. He released one arm, but the touch was immediately back as he put a finger beneath her chin and tipped it upward.

"There is nothing wrong with wanting more, Kelley. Don't think that there is. Wanting more saved my life."

She wanted to ask what that meant, but her heart slammed in her chest. *Mack was more.* The kind of more she'd *never* wanted.

A tip of a finger teased her neck, and she closed her eyes. Never was a long time. And right now she felt completely helpless to do anything but accept his light caress.

His chin dipped the slightest bit so that his lips were close to her temple.

Her chest rose and fell as sensations expanded inside her, shattering the reserve she'd clung to so tightly.

She held her breath, feeling yet again the rise of panic. But he stepped back, looked at her for a long moment.

"God, you're beautiful."

"I'm not."

"Damned near the prettiest thing I've *ever* seen. You look like an angel."

"You're just saying that because of what I just said."

"No, I'm not. I'm telling you what I see. You're just trying to hide her. What I don't understand is why."

She really couldn't breathe now as his low voice seduced her. But the why was stuck in a big painful lump in her chest. It would always be there. He could never know the why.

"Stop hiding. For five minutes stop hiding. I will if you will."

He came forward then, his body barring hers from walking away. Outside, the storm howled, but the warmth of his body cocooned her, solid and warm. Mack raised his hand, grazed her jawline gently.

Everything in her went into a slow meltdown. This gentleness was so foreign, so sensual, she wasn't sure she could bear it. A tiny voice inside of her warned that he'd want more, but she pushed it away with a silent promise to herself of *just this much*. She wanted to see, for once, if she could handle it.

His fingers traced the soft skin, over and over, touching her cheek. Their gazes locked for long moments as she contemplated what would happen next.

"This isn't a good idea," she whispered, hearing the longing in her own voice even as she denied him. And still the tips of his fingers stroked, a tactile kiss against skin. Taking his time.

"I know."

"I think you should go."

"I probably should."

"What do you want from me?" She trembled. She needed different words than she'd heard before. She wanted for once in her adult life to touch and be touched, kiss and be kissed without the mantle of fear cloaking her.

"A kiss," he murmured, his gaze following the path of his fingertips, the whole thing setting her body on fire. "I'd like one kiss."

His fingertips caressed, cupping her cheek as he took the last step in and claimed her mouth.

And oh, he was gentle. Her heart wept with the beauty of it as his soft lips touched hers briefly. Their breaths mingled in the silence as the candle flickered behind them. His lips touched hers again, then moved to graze the crests of her cheekbones. She closed her eyes and sighed. His right hand pulled her closer so that she fit lightly against his body. The sensations were heightened as much by places they didn't touch as the ones where they did.

And still he kissed her, feather-light kisses on her mouth until she finally raised her arms to his shoulders and kissed him back.

Mack closed his eyes against the onslaught of her taste as her fingers dug into his shoulder blades. His blood surged as her mouth opened beneath his, letting him in. He hadn't expected the sweetness, and he hadn't expected the heat. Both hit him like a fist in the gut. And with her small breasts pressed against his chest, he wanted more. One kiss wasn't enough, and the knowledge tore into him, leaving him questioning.

Tonight he'd wanted to kiss her, plain and simple. And not just because she deserved to feel beautiful and have someone mean it, and not because she'd admitted she was afraid of the dark like he was, but because he *wanted* to.

Her body was warm against his and he opened his lips wider, demanding more. A sound growled up from his chest and into her mouth and he took a step forward, backing them against the solid counter.

Kelley felt his body press hers more firmly into the counter. The top dug into her and recalled her to her senses. Not this much. She had to stop it now. She had to keep control of the situation.

She wrenched her lips from his, sliding out from between his body and the Formica countertop.

"We need to stop," she breathed, skittering away to the main part of the room. Once there she realized the only furniture was a bed and she felt the silent scream building. No. She would *not* lose control of the situation. Of herself.

He followed her.

"Kelley."

His tone was placating, but she shook her head. "You've got to go. Now."

"It was just a kiss."

"No, it damn well wasn't," she replied, lifting her head and pinning him with her gaze. "I said no. I meant it."

The words gave her power she hadn't expected. There would be no negotiation. No backing down.

"I don't want to leave you like this."

She fought to keep her voice steady. "I need you to go. Dinner is over."

"All right, if that is what you truly want." He agreed but his tone was harsh and her heart continued to pound away in her chest. He spun on his heel and went to the door, grabbing his jacket on the way.

He was gone with a gust of icy wind and the slam of the door. She rushed behind him and locked it with a click of the dead bolt, adding the chain for good measure.

Then she sat on the bed, touched her lips with shaking fingers. A laugh bubbled up from her belly, high-pitched and disbelieving.

And when it faded away, the only other sound was of her crying.

CHAPTER FOUR

"PULLING OUT?"

Mack was watching her from the doorway to his motel room. At the sound of his voice she closed her eyes, exhaled and pasted a smile on her face as she slammed the passenger door to the truck, wading through several inches of snow to the tailgate. She could handle this. She'd had lots of time to think while the snow had blown and drifted outside. At the end, she'd come to two conclusions. One, she still wanted to make Christmas dinner properly, and for that she needed his help. And two, she had to make it absolutely plain that their relationship was a working one. Cool. Distant. Professional.

"Gram's being released today."

"Oh, that's good news." His words made warmth curl around inside her.

"Yes, it is." She tentatively met his eyes, unable to stop the relief sluicing through her at the good prognosis. "She's doing very well, her doctor says. I think we'll all feel better once she's back home where she belongs."

He leaned against the door frame, looking as if he hadn't a care in the world. His breath made clouds in the cool air, and he had on a jacket but it was unzipped.

"You made it through the storm okay, I see."

Small talk reduced them to redundancies. "Yes," she replied. The word came out softer than she intended as she remembered the long hours she'd sat awake, reliving things she didn't want to again, and finding them all mixed up with how good his kiss had felt. Too good. They'd simply gotten carried away. It was up to her to set things straight. To set the boundaries.

She ran her tongue over her bottom lip as if she could still taste him there. There could be no more kissing if she wanted to achieve her goal. It would only muddy the waters.

"About the dinner…" She leaned against the tailgate and put her hands into her coat pockets. "I want to hire you to teach me to cook Christmas dinner."

She put a slight emphasis on the word *hire*. He had to understand.

"Hire me." He paused. "I already said I'd help you. I don't need your money, Kelley."

"If anyone else hired you, they'd pay you for your time. I am no different." She straightened her spine. This had to be about business only, and he needed to understand that. "Whatever your going rate is, that's fine."

"If this is about the other night…" His shoulder came away from the door frame.

"It's not," she shifted her purse in front of her. He should just stay where he was while she laid out the rules.

"Fair enough. You can hire me to teach you to cook."

She forced herself to lean back against the tailgate of the truck. "Just let me know when I should come to the shop and I'll juggle some things around at home."

He considered for a moment. "It's going to be inconvenient for you, isn't it? Coming into Helena."

She shrugged, though he was right. Driving here and back while trying to keep the Rocking H going and helping out with Gram was going to require some good time management skills. "I'll manage."

"You know, I haven't been out to the Rocking H since I was a kid."

"You want to come to the ranch?" Her back stiffened. In her mind she'd rehearsed this conversation and it had always ended with her in a class at his shop. Not him, in her kitchen. Ever.

"I don't usually do house calls, but it's Christmas." His boyish smile was disarming. He continued on as if she hadn't painted a scowl on her face. "Why not? Save you a drive in. I go out to check on my house at the Ridge several times a week, anyway, it's only a few minutes out of my way."

He made it sound almost like she was doing him the favor. It would make things infinitely easier for her. And Amelia was right next door. She raised one eyebrow. "Are you sure?"

He shifted his weight again, and she was glad he was in his stocking feet, his toes curled over the doorstep.

"You're in a special situation that's all. And you have enough on your plate. Merry Christmas." He sent her a wise-crack smile. "I'm normally a scrooge. You should take advantage of my offer before it disappears."

Her hands fidgeted in the pockets of her coat as she remembered his kiss. It couldn't happen again. She'd thought she could handle it but she couldn't.

"Strictly cooking," she stated baldly, amazed at her own temerity. But they'd danced around it enough. If this were going to happen at her house, it had to be crystal clear.

"Scout's honour." He grinned.

Her shoulders sagged with relief. "I don't know where to start…"

"Leave it to me. I'll come out tomorrow night after my six-o'clock class finishes. We'll tackle your vegetable course."

She paused with her hand on the door handle of the old pickup. Good, safe, vegetables. She'd said what she had to and he'd agreed.

"I live in what used to be the bunkhouse," she explained. "Are you sure this isn't too much of an imposition?"

"I'm sure," he replied. He pushed away from the frame, resting his hand on the edge of the door and looking pleased with himself. "Just be there."

Kelley saw the headlights turn up the drive and stood, taking a nervous breath.

Yesterday she'd been so aware of how she must appear to Mack. When he'd seen her at her truck, she'd been in her customary jeans and plaid shirt, bundled up in a sheepskin jacket. The uniform of a rancher. And it had served her well for a lot of years. She'd never wanted to draw attention to herself. Keeping herself competent and, well, sexless, had worked.

Right up to the point where Mack had kissed her. And called her beautiful.

Maybe he'd meant it, probably he hadn't, but yesterday morning she'd had a sudden desire to look slightly more feminine than a cowpoke in the middle of a roundup. Which hardly made sense since her sole purpose had been to set boundaries.

The vehicle came to a stop outside her door and she brushed a hand down her sweater, smoothing it down. She hadn't wanted to be too obvious, so she'd chosen her best jeans and a soft, thick-knit sweater in tan with a cowl collar. She'd put in earrings, tiny hoops rather than the plain gold studs she normally wore. She tightened her ponytail and took two complete breaths, trying to settle the nerves skittering around in her stomach.

He was here to show her how to cook. It was certainly *not* a date. There was nothing wrong with wanting to look decent rather than like someone who'd just come in from the barn.

She met him on the porch, leaving the door open behind her. He got out of a sport utility and came around the back bumper. Her heart missed a beat, then caught its normal rhythm somewhat accelerated. Lord, he was handsome. The sheepskin collar of his leather jacket cradled his jaw, his breath forming clouds around his head. His dark hair and eyes stood out in the light from her doorway and he paused at the bottom of her steps, holding grocery bags in his hands.

The pause held for only a few seconds, but it was enough that Kelley felt vibrations humming between them. Maybe it hadn't been all in her head. All she knew for sure was that this was the first time in a long time that she was looking forward to spending time with a man. That in itself was an earth-shaking discovery. Once she'd laid out the rules, something had happened to her fear. It had gone into hiding. She'd actually been anticipating his arrival. Maybe because he'd backed off when she'd asked. Or that he'd agreed to her terms without reservation.

"You made it."

His smile lit up his face. "With time to spare."

She found herself returning the easy smile. "Well, you'd better come in. It's cold out."

Kelley stood back as he entered, the grocery bags dangling from his fingers. She reached out and took two, simply to give her hands something to do. It looked as if he'd thought of everything, and she was momentarily intimidated. She was going to look stupid. She'd always considered herself modern, yet the fact that she couldn't cook was something else that made her feel distinctly unfeminine, whether it was wrong or right. It was just there.

No. She would do this. She just had to trust him to show her how.

"Kitchen's through there," she directed. It wasn't as if he'd get lost. She felt her cheeks flush as she followed him. The house was small—a kitchen and living room downstairs, bathroom and bedroom in a loft upstairs. That was all. Four rooms, and a storeroom off the back. She realized how it must look to him. When she'd mentioned his name on the drive from the hospital, Gram had known all about the big fancy house he was building on the bluff. Kelley had kept her eyes on the road, surprised but simply happy Ruby had the energy to make idle chatter.

She started to see the small house through his eyes. She had the main house's cast-off furniture from several years past, and very little in way of decoration. Amelia seemed to have inherited the decorating gene, and when the family got together it was always at the main house.

"Kelley, are you coming or not?"

"Coming!"

She went into the kitchen. He had started unpacking bags and she reached out to help. "Did you bring the whole store?" She was shocked to see the mass of ingredients accumulating on her table.

"It's not as scary as it looks. It's like anything else. Get started, and finish when you're done. Come on…I'll show you how to peel a carrot."

Kelley was pleased he was taking her seriously and keeping things about work. They sat together at the table, companionably peeling potatoes, carrots and chopping something Mack called pancetta.

"It looks like ham. Or thick bacon."

"It is. Kind of. It's not smoked, though. And we'll use the fat from cooking it to flavor the rest of the dish." He reached out to change how she held her knife and she held her breath. The last time he'd touched her this way she'd ended up in his arms. Her fingers shook and she relinquished the knife, took it back when he'd showed her. No more touching; it was too distracting.

"If you say so."

The potatoes, green beans and carrots were all put to boil while he showed her how to fry the pancetta, adding in sage and little bits of red pimiento. This time he didn't cradle her between his arms like he had with the phyllo; it was as if by unspoken agreement they'd decided to maintain their distance. When the pancetta was done, they removed it and cooked lemon, parsley and thyme in another pan. When everything was drained, Mack watched as she poured the lemon parsley mixture over the carrots, then put the beans to sauté lightly as she mashed the potatoes. With a growing sense of satisfaction, she measured out sour cream, cream cheese, butter and milk and added them to the smooth potatoes, then added the pancetta mixture to the beans all under the tutelage of Mack's keen eye.

"Oh, my word." Kelley looked around at her kitchen. Pots were everywhere. Potato and carrot peelings were still on the table. And she suddenly realized that despite the apparent success of the recipes, she had no serving dishes for anything.

"What's wrong?" He moved to her elbow. "You did wonderfully. Far better than I would have expected, considering the asparagus puffs disaster. We didn't even need a fire extinguisher."

She stared up at him, feeling slightly shell-shocked. "It's not that. I'm not ready for this. Look at my kitchen. If I make a mess like this in Amelia's kitchen, she'll…"

He pushed her into a chair and smiled indulgently. "First, you're going to breathe."

"I've finally bitten off more than I can chew."

"You haven't. You run a ranch nearly single-handedly, in charge of how many men and head of cattle? Come on. A single dinner isn't going to be your downfall."

"Yes, but I know how to do that."

"Well, you weren't born knowing how to run a ranch. You know because you learned. Three days ago you were shredding phyllo. Tonight you've made lemon parsleyed carrots, green beans with pancetta and sage, and delicious mashed potatoes." His hand grazed her knee, leaving a trail of warmth. "You're just overwhelmed, that's all. Now that you're getting the hang of things, you'll be able to tidy as you go. Relax, and let me bring you a plate."

Kelley absently rubbed the spot he'd patted as he removed a pan from the oven and sliced an herb-crusted turkey breast he'd brought with him. When the plate was full, he brought it to her. "Taste that and believe."

Where he got his confidence in her, she had no idea. Tonight was a small battle in a big war in her opinion. She picked up her fork as Mack cleaned the table of their peelings. "Aren't you eating?"

"I'm making room. Go ahead, tell me what you think."

"I don't want to ruin it. It's so pretty." The potatoes were snowy white, contrasted with the vibrant orange and green of the other vegetables. The smell of the turkey breast had her stomach growling. She took her first bite of beans and her eyes widened. "It's good. I mean, really good!"

"Of course it is. And you did it. I just watched and offered guidance."

He sat down with his own plate.

And the room got very quiet.

Kelley suddenly realized that for the second time in a week they were sharing a meal.

"This feels weird."

"You'll get over it." He aimed another winning smile her way. How was it that he was so relaxed when she was completely tied up in knots, just from being near him?

The trouble was, Kelley *was* getting over it. She was starting to like him. Unlike the rough, domineering men she was used to, he didn't judge. Mack's patience and careful guidance gave her confidence. He hadn't questioned her "rules," and his easy-going manner had a way of inspiring her trust. If this was the true Mack, then she also knew he was very good at what he did. No wonder he'd made Mack's Kitchen such a success.

He'd done things that she'd only daydreamed about. She still resented it the tiniest bit, knowing he'd seen so much of the world while she'd been held here by an invisible leash. But it was hard to hate him for it when they were sitting in her kitchen, eating a meal he'd helped her cook. He didn't look like a millionaire. He looked like an ordinary guy in jeans and a sweater who just happened to be, perhaps, the best-looking man she'd ever known.

"Can I ask you a question?"

"Sure." He scooped up potatoes on his fork and took a bite. "You did a really good job with these, you know."

His praised warmed her. "Thank you."

"What's your question?"

She looked up, feeling suddenly shy. "You've traveled so much. I was just wondering…what's Paris like?"

"Paris?"

"I've…I've just never traveled."

He was quiet for a few moments, as if trying to decide.

"Paris is noisy and hectic and smelly. Of course, it's easy to love when it smells of the day's fresh bread, or when you're walking the Left Bank and you're assaulted with exotic scents from the restaurants and cafés. It rains like the devil and then the clouds open up and it's like beams of light from heaven." He grinned. "Of course, no trip is complete without visiting the palace at Versailles. And you can really see why the revolution happened."

"Let them eat cake?"

His low laugh warmed her clear to her toes. "Precisely."

"And you've been to Italy? London?" She was hungry for the information now and leaned forward, encouraging him with a swoop of her fork.

He leaned back in his chair, toying with his glass of water.

"Of course. I spent a month eating my way through towns and markets in Tuscany. And London is just…London. I lived in Chelsea for a while. Sunday mornings we…I went walking in Battersea Park and drank cappuccino from a paper cup."

"It sounds wonderful."

"Christmas in London is like nowhere else." He smiled, but his eyes took on a faraway look, and the curve of his lips faltered the smallest bit.

Did the memory hold some sadness for him? She wanted to ask, but it felt presumptuous. Besides, to do so would go against the "rules" she'd set up. Cool. Distant. Professional.

Trouble was, the more they talked, the less distant she became.

"What's it like at Christmas, then?"

He sat back in his chair, his face taking on a faraway look again. "There's skating at Somerset House, the lights in the West End. Then there's the Christmas tree in Trafalgar Square and carolers…"

"Why did you come back?"

"Because this is home, Kelley." He met her eyes with quiet acceptance.

"But you have no one here."

The moment it was out of her mouth she wished she could take it back. Everyone in town knew that his mother had skipped off right after Mack had finished high school. Even though she'd barely known Mack, the story had caused a sensation in Rebel Ridge. His gaze slid away from hers and he picked up his glass of water. What had possessed her to point out he was alone…a week before Christmas?

She started to reach out but drew her hand back. She still wasn't comfortable touching him. "I'm sorry, Mack," she offered. "That was insensitive."

"It's okay. It's true."

She saw the line of his lips and the set of his jaw and knew she'd touched a nerve.

"How's your grandmother?"

She let him change the subject because clearly he was uncomfortable. The sudden realization he was going to be alone for Christmas settled in an empty place inside her. She had Gram, and Amelia and Jesse. But Mack had no one. For the briefest of moments, "Why don't you join us" hovered on her tongue. But she couldn't bring herself to say the words. Inviting someone for Christmas…well it was a family holiday. After the kiss they'd shared—she really didn't want it to be misconstrued. She wouldn't lead him on when nothing could come of it. And Lord only knew what Amelia and Gram would make of her inviting a man to Christmas dinner. So she kept the words inside and answered his question instead.

"She's doing well, but a bit slower. She tries not to show it, but when she thinks no one is looking…" Kelley wrinkled her brow. She couldn't help the worry. "She's not one to take it easy. I wish she'd be more patient. Let herself heal properly."

"If she's like I remember, she always went a mile a minute."

"Not now. And she's lost weight. She insists it's the hospital food, but I know better. She's getting old, Mack. Nothing we can do to stop it, but it sure doesn't make it any easier. She raised us. And she's the only family we have left."

Mack leaned forward and put a warm hand on her knee beneath the table. "You obviously care for your family deeply. And they love you. I know she's ailing, but I envy you that, Kelley. I envy it very much."

All of her senses were focused on the warm spot his hand made on her leg. Normally she shied away from physical touches.

But normally there was no Mack. And he seemed to touch like it was the most natural thing in the world.

"You do? But you've done so much with your life."

"Yes, I have. And I never had to answer to anyone, either. There's something to be said for that."

"But?"

He smiled. "So you did sense the *but*."

Kelley wasn't sure if he realized it or not, but his thumb was drawing lazy circles on her leg. She should move it away, but it felt good. It didn't feel threatening. It felt right.

Finally his voice came low, and maybe with a trace of anger she hadn't heard before.

"Not everyone grows up that way. In my line of work, I see a lot of families that don't work. For whatever reason. People who are alone. Divorcees. Singles. Widowers. All searching for something. You came to me to help your family. You came to me because you wanted to give something, not to find it. You're the exception, Kelley."

She didn't feel like the exception, and didn't feel like she was much of a giver, either. She was trying to hold things together, that was all. Trying to show she could do it, that there was more to her than what people saw at face value. But she couldn't go into all that with him. She'd feel even more foolish if he knew that one of her reasons was to feel more feminine.

"It's getting late," she murmured, trying hard to slow her heart rate down. His hand was still touching her thigh. It was silly to let a simple touch affect her so much. She pushed away from the table and gathered the plates. "Thank you, Mack. Now I have an appetizer, and I can manage the vegetables. I think. Although I have no idea what to do with what's left over."

"I can take it away if you want. If you have any plastic containers."

What on earth would he want her leftovers for? He was a cook, for goodness' sake! Surely he'd want to cook his own food from fresh ingredients.

"I have a place I donate to regularly. Having a cooking school means sometimes there's a surplus. If it means someone gets a decent meal, or any meal at all…"

Kelley looked up into his eyes. Mack Dennison was turning out to be a continual source of surprise. There was no putting on airs with him, despite the flashy SUV and the brand-name clothing. "You're turning out to be a bit of a saint," she said lightly, while emotions within her churned.

"Hardly a saint," he murmured, taking advantage of her full hands and moving in to kiss her.

CHAPTER FIVE

KELLEY'S FINGERS tightened around the plates as Mack's lips on hers made everything in her body turn to jelly. It was the most delicious thing in the world. Like the perfect ending to a long day.

His fingers were firm on her upper arms and his body warm against hers. He took a step and she danced slowly backward with him until her hips met with the countertop. Then there was no give between their bodies at all. His was firm and strong. And heaven help her, she liked it. It made her feel protected, not in danger.

The kiss broke off, and his forehead rested against hers, his breath fanning her cheeks and doing nothing to relieve the unexpected vibrations humming through her body.

"I told myself I wasn't going to do that." His voice was ragged and rough, sexy enough to make her toes curl.

"It's okay," she whispered, realizing that it truly was. The air still crackled between them; the admission had done nothing to defuse the moment. If anything, she wanted him more. His apology told her he'd respected her boundaries. He'd pulled back rather than pushing for more, and she was just feminine enough to be flattered that he'd wanted to kiss her again despite his good intentions.

She turned to the side and deposited the dishes beside the sink. She had to take a mental step back. She wasn't prepared for him and was even less ready for the feelings that suddenly were cropping up. Anticipation. Desire. She didn't know what to do with that. She was used to being in charge, but that was work. Her personal life…well, she didn't exactly have a personal life, and it shocked her that for the first time in ages she actually wanted one. If she hadn't, then why had she made an effort to dress up tonight? And yet still, deep down, fear tried to claw its way out, along with a certainty that she wasn't ready to take this relationship past friendship.

"I can't," she murmured, attempting to squirm out from between his body and the cupboards. She was fighting a ghost that shouldn't matter anymore, and she resented it. Mack made her not want it to matter at all.

She wished she could read his eyes as he watched her so closely, but she didn't have a clue of what he was thinking. He must think her the most irritating woman; she knew she was blowing hot and cold. She'd get just so close and then push away. She could still feel the heat of his hands on her skin and she swallowed.

She ached to be touched again but something held her back. There was a big gap between moving past fear and into trust territory; too large a gap to leap across. "Could we just be friends, please? I'm not looking to get involved."

"As I recall, you were kissing me, too."

His dark eyes were unwavering. He put his hands in his jeans pockets, and she wanted to wrap her arms around his ribs and snuggle in. Somehow he made her feel safe, and perhaps that was the most dangerous thing of all.

"I know." She could do this; she dealt with stubborn old ranch hands every day. She took a breath. "I need your help. I don't think I can pull a Christmas dinner off without it. But if we get involved…it will make a mess of things." She tried to think of it in terms he could relate to. "We're keeping the dishes I make simple, right? Let's just keep *us* the same way. If we make it too complicated…"

His dark eyes probed hers. "You're scared. Don't be. Kelley, friends can kiss. There are no rules against it. But we can take it slow if you want."

She would get through this, she would, and with some shred of dignity. Her hands were cold and she rubbed the damp palms on her jeans. "We agreed to a professional relationship. I'd rather we stayed just…friends. I like having you as a friend, Mack."

Mack clenched his fingers within the denim pockets of his jeans, simply to keep from reaching out and touching her. He'd already broken his first rule—never get involved with a client. There'd been something about her in the motel room, though, a soft vulnerability he found irresistible. She kissed him as though she meant it but then backed off. She had the other night, too, and he'd known he had to back away. Why was she afraid? And what was it about her that kept drawing him in, making him try again?

"The more I'm with you, the harder it is to be just your friend," he said honestly.

Her eyes widened further, but not with the desire he craved. Once again he saw the flash of fear. Why in the world would she be afraid of him? His hand slid out of his pocket and he took the steps necessary to reach her and take her hand, wanting to reassure her. He lifted it to his cheek and pressed a small kiss to the back. Her hand was cold, and questions popped into his head. "I know something's going on with you. But…everyone has wounds, Kelley."

Kelley flinched, but didn't break eye contact. Pain, humiliation, self-loathing, disgust…she remembered those feelings well enough, and they had crippled her for years. Now, when she really wanted to move past them, she felt angry that they still held her back.

And she sure as hell couldn't tell him why.

"Even you?" She let him keep her fingers within his. The contact was strangely soothing.

"Even me."

He hesitated, and she got the sense he was picking and choosing what to tell and what not to. She'd done it often enough herself. Measuring words, avoiding eye contact until a decision had been made. She knew he'd chosen his words when he looked fully into her face.

"Let's just say, not everyone has an ideal upbringing. And things happen that color their lives. Things happen that you cannot change or take back."

His words struck a painful chord with her. But she knew he

wouldn't understand this. Even after a decade, she found it impossible to understand. "It doesn't matter."

He sighed. "If you ever want to talk about it, let me know. I'm here."

She felt as if his dark eyes could see clear through her and accepted her for who she was. That in itself was a novelty. Somehow they'd ended up not only kissing but, more important, talking.

He stacked the last container of leftovers, preparing to leave. "I just want you to know that I think what you're trying to do for your family is a good thing."

She shook her head. "This is no big sacrifice on my part. I love them."

"You're the glue holding the family together, Kelley. If I can see it, I hope they can, too."

Kelley blinked furiously at the unsolicited praise. It was inconceivable that she was the glue. She was just Kelley who ran the ranch.

He was going to be alone at Christmas. It ceased to matter what Amelia or Gram would say. She would explain. They would understand—no one should spend the holidays alone.

She leaned forward, holding out one hand in invitation. "Why don't you come to Christmas dinner?"

He balanced the containers while shock glimmered on his face. "You're inviting me to your family dinner?"

"Do you have somewhere else you need to be?"

He didn't answer right away, and she suddenly realized maybe she'd been presumptuous. Maybe he did have someplace special to go.

"I'm not a charity case, Kelley. I don't want you to ask me because I told you I was alone. I'm fine. The last thing I want is for you to feel obligated."

She smiled. Pride, she understood. "Heck, I'm not obligated. I'm paying you for your time. This is off the clock and offered in friendship, Mack. Nothing more. Come to dinner with friends."

He blinked twice. "I'd be honored to come."

"Honored?" It was an unexpected compliment. No one ever

seemed "honored" when she did something. She was struck again by the gentleness in his voice.

"Maybe it beats sitting in a motel room by myself watching *It's a Wonderful Life*."

He tried to make light, but she could see through it. "Will you see your mom over the holidays?"

"You know my mom left Rebel Ridge a long time ago." His lips were set in a way that let her know the subject was closed. "I'm spending Christmas Eve at the shelter, serving dinner. And Christmas afternoon—" he paused, his eyes skittered away from hers for a moment "—at a rehab centre in Helena."

He had no one, and spent his holiday with others who had no one, too. The absolute loneliness struck Kelley square in the chest. As long as she could remember, they'd had presents and a special family breakfast, winding up with a traditional Christmas dinner. Stockings were hung and old Bing Crosby carols played. The very thought of someone spending the holiday without any of that was impossible.

"Then I'm very glad you're joining us."

He cleared his throat. "Me, too.

Wordlessly he gathered up his leftovers and went to the door. She followed him and held it open as he shrugged into his jacket. They'd just come to an agreement, so why on earth was he feeling as though everything was suddenly more out of control?

At the bottom of the steps he turned to find her standing in the doorway again, the glow from the porch light shining off her hair. With her soft smile, she reminded him of an angel. His heart skipped as she raised a hand in farewell.

He lifted his own and went to his truck, his breath forming clouds in the chilly air. Maybe he should have told her the whole truth. But they'd forged a friendship tonight, and the last thing he wanted to do was endanger it. In the long run, it wouldn't make any difference.

He started the truck and looked back at the house. She had gone inside out of the cold, and the door was shut. As he put the truck in reverse, he wished for the first time in a long time that it wouldn't make any difference at all.

* * *

"Easy. Shhh." Kelley held Risky's halter while Mack stayed outside the stall, quietly watching. "I'm sorry, Dr. Laramie. He's usually not this jumpy." Dr. Cooper, the regular vet, was on holidays. Andrew Laramie was his locum, filling in. Risky could sense a stranger despite Laramie's patient and soothing voice.

It had been three days since the kissing incident in her kitchen. Today Mack had brought the small turkey as promised for a practice run. They had worked companionably, preparing the turkey and stuffing and putting it in the oven. They'd bantered and teased. As friends. And yet…she wished he'd look at her *that* way again.

He was in her thoughts all the time. As she took care of stock, checked fences, supervised the hands, he was there on the fringes of her mind, with his casual touches, ready smile, soft seductive kisses. She didn't want to, and hadn't seen it coming, but she was falling for him.

But all of that had fled her mind with Risky's emergency. She'd had her hands full of soapy water when one of the hands had arrived at the door saying Risky'd been cut. She'd dropped everything in the kitchen and rushed to the barn, Mack right on her heels. She'd had the big bay gelding since she was fifteen. And when she saw the blood seeping from the gash, she knew stitches were the best plan.

Dr. Laramie gritted his teeth. "I'd rather not sedate unless it's necessary. But I think he should be stitched, and for that I'm going to have to."

Risky tossed his head once more. "Risky. Hush now."

Her muscles ached from keeping a firm hold on the halter. Even though Risky was cross-tied in his stall, his agitation meant Laramie couldn't make his sutures. For a moment she considered letting the wound go, letting it heal on its own. She met the vet's eyes and asked the question silently.

"It's up to you. It's deep enough to stitch but you could get away with it. Just."

Kelley turned away. Mack was watching her steadily, yet with a vigilance that made her feel as though he'd be there if she needed him. He didn't step in, didn't offer an opinion. His implied confidence in her was a rarity. Most often the men she knew would either be telling her what they would do or disregarding her altogether. That Mack didn't, said as much about him as it did about her.

She looked back at Risky and gave his neck a reassuring rub. She hated sedation. There was something about making a creature so vulnerable that she resisted.

"No, you're right. If you're going to stitch he needs sedation." A vicious jerk left her shoulder aching.

As the vet prepared the needles required, she tried to calm Risky. But his eyes were wild and she knew he was afraid and everything she did seemed to make it worse.

"He knows you're scared for him." Mack's voice was soft in her ear, but sure. His warm breath sent tingles down her body. "Let me try."

She stood back, relinquishing her hold on the halter. She could use the few moments to rest her arms. "Let me know when you have had enough. He's strong."

He didn't touch the halter at all but held out his hand, palm up. Risky sniffed, nudged. Mack stepped in and stroked the horse's jaw. And Kelley heard him muttering words, words she couldn't make out, but Risky stopped jumping and skittering. The whites of his eyes disappeared and the anxious stamping of hooves gentled. Dr. Laramie waited only a few moments. Standing perfectly still, eyes fastened on Mack, Risky received the medication with merely a twitch of his hide.

Mack placed his hands on Risky's head and rubbed softly, uttering soft words while he blinked rapidly. He hadn't expected such a complete reaction…not within the horse and definitely not within himself. He'd merely wanted to try—he'd seen Kelley's wince of pain as she struggled to hold the horse's head.

She had more on her plate than he'd initially realized, and he also knew there was something holding her back. She'd been so jumpy after a few simple kisses. He wanted her to trust him with more than a dinner. And the simple truth was that the gelding was afraid and in pain. It reminded Mack of the many times he'd been the same way. And how much work it had been to pull himself out. If Risky could trust him, then perhaps Kelley would, too.

"Mack…"

"Shhh," he uttered, ignoring Kelley, softly stroking Risky's muzzle as the drugs took hold. For a moment he felt an undeniable sadness that the animal had to be sedated. Turned into a ghost of itself, numb against the pain. Mack had lived that way far too long, without even the benefit of drugs or alcohol. And as he finally met Kelley's eyes across the stall, he knew it was time to start living again.

"How did you do that?"

The glow of approval on her face made him feel ten feet tall. He looked at Risky and murmured, "He just needed someone to talk to." He paused. "How's the vet doing?"

"I'm halfway there, thanks," came the voice from deeper in the stall. "Won't be long now."

Still Mack stroked softly, murmuring reassurances to the animal as Laramie put in the sutures.

When the stitching was done, Kelley watched as Mack relinquished his hold on Risky and stepped out of the stall, back into the corner once again. She listened with only half an ear as Laramie gave her instructions for caring for the wound—it was all things she knew already. What she really wanted to know was how did Mack know how to calm a frantic horse? And why was she just seeing this side of him now?

Watching him talk to Risky had sent a wave of love over her she could scarcely comprehend. In that moment he'd been different. He'd been tall and strong and capable and a man that she felt somehow she could lean on. He was just Mack. He'd dominated Risky with kindness and not force. Would he be that gentle with her? Her eyes had fixated on his hands, softly stroking, soothing. Would his hands be equally as tender on her skin? It was a revelation to her that she even desired it. That she was considering taking that leap after so many years celibate, and with a man she'd known such a short time. Time had ceased to matter, because in her heart she felt she could trust him. She didn't want to be just friends. Up until this moment it had seemed the only option. But maybe, just maybe, Mack had changed all of that.

She blinked, took a step back, collecting scraps of bandage for the garbage. And then what? Where could they possibly go together? She thought about her sister and how she'd rushed into a relationship, had her heart broken by Jesse's father, and how difficult it had been being a single mother. She'd fallen for this Boone she'd hired and he'd gone, too. She thought of her own history and the weight it would bring to a new relationship. She was being fanciful. And there was no time for that.

Dr. Laramie was shaking Mack's hand when she turned back around.

"Thanks for your help."

"No problem." Mack looked more at home in the barn than Kelley could have imagined. With his jeans and heavy jacket, he could have been one of the hands helping out.

"Just a question," the vet asked. "How did you learn to do that? He responded very well to you."

Mack laughed. "I used to work at a farm outside Rebel Ridge. I always had a soft spot for the horses. Why?"

Laramie bent to grab his case. "I'm only filling in for Cooper while he has Christmas with his family. After that…well, I'm going home myself. A ranch in Alberta," he continued. "It's going to take a few months to get the details straightened out, but I'm setting up a rescue operation. I spent a lot of time working with Thoroughbreds, and it's really hard watching them be put down when their run is done. Or seeing an animal that's been abused. I had enough and quit. We could use a few guys like you. You have a real way."

"Thoroughbreds…wait, Andrew Laramie. You worked with racehorses, didn't you?"

Laramie nodded. "That's right."

"I remember you…. I think it was the Breeder's Cup last year. I was there watching with several of our investors."

It was a reminder that Mack lived in a world different from the Rocking H. Different from hers. Kelley aimed a bright smile at Laramie. "Mack is more than a ranch hand."

She made the declaration with a certain sense of pride. She

wouldn't have done that a few weeks ago. She *was* proud of him, she discovered. He was good at what he did, and successful. It couldn't have been easy, not when he started from nothing, no matter what he said. "He owns the Mack's Kitchen franchises."

Andrew grinned. "I know someone who'd love to do what you do, Mack. Personally, I don't know the right end of a spatula."

"Our newest location is opening up in Washington in January. I'm heading up there for the launch. We're always looking for franchising opportunities."

Kelley looked at her feet as the three of them walked down the corridor to the doors. He really would be leaving, then. After such a short time, she was getting used to having him around. Mack's arm brushed hers as Laramie laughed lightly.

"Might be difficult. *She* lives north of the border. Owns the bakery in Larch Valley and makes the best brownies I ever tasted." His mouth twisted. "Then there's the tiny problem that she won't speak to me."

Mack's fingers found hers and squeezed. She couldn't look at him. If she did, he'd know how much a simple handclasp affected her. It made her feel part of a couple, and that was a novelty. She'd been on her own so long it was a revelation to be a part of a united front. In the back of her mind she knew he would be going back to his life after Christmas. In her heart, at this moment, it didn't matter.

"Well, good luck with that," Mack offered. "Setting up a ranch can't be anywhere near as hard as thawing a woman's heart."

Laramie sent him a significant look. "Amen, brother."

She bit her lip. Did Mack think she needed thawing? She knew it was true. She knew she'd closed herself off for too long. What he didn't know is that he'd already thawed the ice around her heart. Could she show him that and still have her heart intact when he was gone?

Laramie raised a hand in a wave and strode off to his truck, while Mack and Kelley stood in the frosty air outside the barn.

Kelley sighed, looking up at the crystal-blue sky—a sharp

contrast to the pristine snow. Seeing Mack here, comfortable in her world, only made the attraction to him stronger. Was it so wrong to want to grab on to any bit of happiness, even if it was only for now?

"Kel?"

She turned to look up at him, saw his dark eyes twinkling back, saw a hint of stubble on his jaw that made her want to run her fingertips along the roughness.

"Hmmm?"

"Has it occurred to you that we left a turkey in the oven?"

"Oh, no!"

Together they sprinted through the snow to the house, and Kelley flung open the door. There was no smoke, but an acrid odour wafted out of the kitchen, and she ran forward with a cry.

"Wait!" Mack commanded. He bustled through, opening the back door and windows first. "Let me."

He reached into the oven as thin tendrils of smoke came out. Kelley pressed her fingers to her lips as she tried not to laugh at the sight. It wasn't all funny. She had a dinner in a few days, and the trial run for the main event was a disaster. But the look on Mack's face…a giggle escaped.

He put the roaster on the stovetop and stared at it. Kelley found him as sexy in a pair of oven mitts as she had when he'd held Risky's halter. Maybe more so.

"If my partners saw this—" he shook his head "—they'd be backing out in a hurry."

"Andrew Laramie would give you a job."

He angled a wry look in her direction. "Ha-ha."

Kelley stepped forward, picked up a fork and poked at the bird. "Yep. Definitely done."

"You're not upset."

She smiled. "Oh, Mack, this is one time I couldn't care less."

"But I thought…"

And as the words hung in the air, something clicked into place. For the first time, she was completely comfortable with a man. She trusted him. The dinner didn't matter. Nothing mattered, except feeling free for the first time. He had done that. Just by being him.

In this moment the past ceased to exist, and as it melted away so did the terror, the uncertainty, all of it. He had been careful with her from the start. She'd seen his hands, his wide, big hands so gentle on Risky's halter today, his voice soft and soothing. He was a man who understood pain and hurt and regret, and she knew without a doubt that she could trust him.

The Christmas CD they'd put in the stereo was still playing, over and over, and it no longer mattered what might happen in the future. She didn't care that they were from different worlds. He was here now. It was almost Christmas. If ever there was a time to take a chance, it was in this moment.

In the space of a heartbeat, she pressed her body against his, her lips on his lips.

She opened her mouth, meeting him equally. For once she felt blessed to be tall as their curves fit together like nesting eggs, his frame only a few inches ahead of hers. His kiss was like all the best things of Christmas—candlelight and ginger-bread and the excitement of waking at four in the morning to open presents. She smiled against his mouth and found the hem of his sweater, snuck her hands underneath it and spread them wide over the heated skin of his back, marveling at the smooth strength of it.

He broke off the kiss, breathing heavily. "You said you wanted—"

"I changed my mind."

"Why?"

She leaned back far enough so she could see his face. He meant it. He really meant it. He wasn't pushing, but asking permission in his own way. Her heart soared with the realization.

"Because I want you, all of you." The words came out, filled the room, filled her heart because she meant them.

"You want me."

The indecision in his voice tore at her heart. Had no one ever wanted him before? It was inconceivable. His dark eyes clung to hers, tacitly asking—he was a man who would always ask, never take.

Never before had she felt sexually powerful, but she did now. She ran her tongue over her bottom lip, suddenly so sure that it almost made her laugh with the joy of it. The freedom was energizing. "I want you. I want all of you."

If she thought he'd hesitate further, she was wrong. His hand, his very capable hand, the one that had calmed her horse and made delicate pastry in a dingy motel room, now cupped her neck firmly as he dragged her close again. His fingers deftly slid her buttons through the buttonholes and she held her breath as he pushed the shirt off her shoulders. But none of the gut-knotting fear came. Only intense pleasure and anticipation.

His sweater joined her shirt on the floor and their skin was pressed together, hot and firm and oh, so wonderful without the barrier of fabric between them. She took his hand and led him upstairs to the loft, shaking a little as she realized what she was asking. She was asking him to make love to her, and it was exhilarating and terrifying all at once.

"Do you have protection?"

"You don't?"

He couldn't possibly know how silly that question was. Of course she didn't have anything resembling birth control; there'd never been any need. But rather than say it and ruin what progress they'd made, she answered simply. "No, I don't." And hoped he did.

He slid his wallet from his jeans and withdrew a foil packet. "I have one."

"For emergencies?" She raised an eyebrow, surprised at her own temerity.

His responding grin was dangerously sexy. "Exactly."

She lifted her chin, suddenly realizing she was standing before him in her underwear and that his hungry eyes were taking in every inch of her bare skin. She pushed away the shyness threatening to take over and smiled softly. "And this is an emergency?"

Dark eyes glittered at her. "Oh, honey, you've no idea."

He took a step forward, but she stopped him once more. In one way she was teasing, but in another found she wanted to know. "How long has that been in there?"

And as he reached for her, he growled, "Long enough."

CHAPTER SIX

MACK CLOSED HIS EYES, savoring the feeling and the taste of her that lingered in his mouth. Right now Kelley's head rested on his chest, her blond hair falling over her face and her arm looped around his midsection. She was sleeping; he could tell by the slow, hot breaths that dampened his chest.

Lord, she'd been sweet. And fairly innocent, he was sure. It was in the way she touched, with a hint of shy hesitancy, like she wanted him to take the lead. It had been fresh, like a spring rain. The women he knew weren't like that. But Kelley...

He sighed, closed his eyes, feeling her warmth curled around him. He hadn't wanted to care about a woman for a very long time. Not since Christmas two years ago. That was when everything had changed. Oh, he'd believed once. But it had been a hard lesson to learn.

Her arm tightened around his ribs and he held his breath, not wanting to disturb her. He'd let things go this far and he shouldn't have. Now he'd gone and spent the night—another rule broken. He rubbed a hand over the stubble on his face. And yet he couldn't find it within himself to regret it. That in itself set off alarm bells in his head. It was well and good for her to need his help. It wasn't good when he started feeling attached.

"Mack?" She said his name in a husky whisper that reached right to the middle of him and grabbed.

"What, Kelley?"

And damned if she didn't laugh, a low, sexy rumble that came right from her toes and out her heart.

"That was good, Mack."

He smiled, lifted his head and kissed her hair, determined not to ruin the morning. "I know."

"No, I mean really good. Better than I expected."

He couldn't stop the smile that spread on to his face. "You gotta stop setting your expectations low…"

She laughed, a sexy little sound that did funny things to his insides. "I'm glad you stayed."

Suddenly he was, too. Even if it did complicate things more than he was strictly comfortable with.

"Do you want coffee?"

"Mmmm. You making it?"

"Sure."

She snuggled into him and he felt other parts of his body wake up. He had to move now, or they'd never get out of bed. And he didn't think a repeat of last night was the best of plans.

"I'll be back in a few minutes."

When he came back, mugs in hand, she'd fallen asleep again, her hair and the sheets a sexy tangle. He wet his lips, wondering what the hell he'd been thinking. It wasn't the sex. It was Kelley, and the fact that he cared about her—too much. Right now he wanted to gather her up in his arms and hold her close—every soft, sweet-scented inch of her.

That hadn't been part of the plan. He should have known better than to spend the night. He cleared his throat. "Your coffee, madam."

Kelley dragged herself out of sleep, propelled by the amazing smell. She blinked, opened her eyes, and saw Mack sitting on the edge of the bed, smiling and holding out a mug of steaming brew.

"Good morning." She moved to sit up and froze.

She was naked! And here was Mack in his jeans and shirt, partly unbuttoned so she could see a generous slice of the hard chest beneath it. She dimly remembered waking a while ago, snuggling into his body. Her face flamed. In the bright light of morning, the magnitude of what they'd done hit her with full force. She'd had sex. With Mack Dennison. She put her hands to her red face and Mack laughed.

"That's charming," he said. He still held the coffee out and she wanted it...badly. She could hide her blushing face behind the mug. How was a woman supposed to act the morning after? She had no idea. Her sum total experience had been limping home from prom and hiding her soiled dress in the back of the closet until she could burn it.

Holding the quilt to her chest, she wiggled until she was sitting in the bed, and reached for the mug.

She took a hot sip and closed her eyes. Delicious. When she opened them, Mack leaned over and kissed her gently. Chaste, if it came down to it. If it could be chaste, considering what had passed between them last night.

"I'll make us some breakfast." Mack reached for his coffee that he'd put on the dresser. She tried not to be disappointed that he didn't crawl under the covers with her.

"I'm awfully glad you're here." Her heart blossomed as she realized how true it was. "And I'm so pleased you're spending Christmas with us. Amelia has the most beautiful tree. And her pecan pie...you haven't lived until you've had her pie."

A shadow passed over his face and Kelley frowned. What had she said that was wrong? She sensed defiance in the set of his jaw, but more than that. Hurt. Her heart melted just a little bit knowing it.

She held the covers to her chest with her arms and put her free hand on his wrist, feeling the pulse there thrum beneath her fingers. "What is it? What did I say?"

He raised his head and she stared into his eyes. She could so easily get lost in the chocolaty depths of them.

He turned his hand over and twined his fingers with hers. "When you talk about Christmas..."

Her breath held. Was he going to back out? Was it too much too soon? She hadn't planned any of this. And she was pretty sure he hadn't, either.

"I don't really talk about this, but when you speak of the holidays and traditions and that sort of thing...well, you should know I've never had a real Christmas."

"Never?"

"Never."

"No tree, turkey and presents?"

He laughed, a bitter, jerky sound. "Not ever. Not even close. My holidays normally consist of tasteful trees in a hotel lobby and a dinner in a five-star restaurant."

She couldn't imagine December twenty-fifth coming and going without a proper celebration. Her heart ached for the childhood magic he must have missed. "That's the loneliest thing I've ever heard. I don't understand."

Mack knew it was better that she know the truth now. He had no illusions about the so-called magic of the season, didn't go in for the sappy sentimentality of peace on earth and good will toward men. In his house, there'd never been Santa Claus or dinners or magic of any sort. Why start now, only for himself?

There'd always been a little voice in the back of his mind saying he hadn't deserved it. In his head, he knew that wasn't true. But in his heart, where it mattered, he'd never been able to shake the thought completely.

He'd tried once, and had failed utterly. He knew there was always a crash at the end of the buildup. It was better that she know the truth now. He wasn't who she thought he was.

"There was never money for Christmas—or much desire to put in the effort, either. Not when the priority is making sure there's enough vodka in the house to get through the season. That's what happens when you grow up with an alcoholic."

"Your mother?"

He heard the gasp that accompanied the explanation and hated it. "That's right," he confirmed. He hooked his thumbs in the tabs of his pockets. "A drunk who cared more about her next bottle than feeding her kid."

"I never guessed…"

She met his gaze; he challenged her with his eyes. "No one did."

"Oh, Mack, how awful for you." Her eyes softened and he tried very hard to hate her for pitying him. "So you really never had Christmas when you were a boy?"

He looked away, determined not to feel like the little lost boy any longer. He'd grown up. Made a success of himself. "She tried a few times. It just never quite worked out in a *White Christmas* sort of way, you know? And now…there doesn't seem to be a point. It's just me, and with the business, it's our busiest retail season. The closest I get is decking out the stores and bringing in seasonal stock."

"I'm sorry, Mack. About your mom. About all of it."

He hadn't wanted to delve further into his past, but he'd rather she walked away now before either of them got in too deep. "I took home ec so I could learn to feed myself. By the time I was a teenager, I had a teenager's appetite. And boxed mac and cheese can only fill a kid's stomach for so long."

"Oh, Mack." She sighed his name, lifted their joined hands and placed a kiss on the back of his thumb.

He shifted on the covers, pulling his hand out of her grasp. "You see? That's why I didn't tell you before. Now you pity me. And I don't want your pity. I never wanted anyone's pity."

"Can't I feel sorry for the boy?"

His anger flared. "No. That boy doesn't exist anymore. I discovered I liked cooking. I was good at it. I got a job at a farm after school and on weekends and used my wages to put food on my own table. Later I used the money to study. And I got backing to open my first Mack's Kitchen."

"Then why so angry? Why so secretive? No one would think any less of you…"

He's teeth clenched almost painfully as he heard sympathy in her voice. "Don't you?" he bit out. "Don't you see me differently now?"

"Yes. I see you as a kid who overcame a lot of odds to make a success of himself." She readjusted the sheet and leaned close to him, forcing him to look at her. "There's no shame in that, Mack. It's admirable."

"I don't want the past to define me. I want the present. The future."

"And it does. Look at how well you've done."

"Stop, please."

"Did you think people would think less of you if they knew? That I would?"

That's exactly what he'd thought. Plus he'd started having

to deal with publicity because of the success of the stores. The last thing he wanted was to capitalize on his childhood woes. Some things should remain private.

"I didn't want those days to be used to sell a product. I refuse to let my life be a rags-to-riches sob story."

Kelley smiled softly. She wasn't patronizing him, or indulging him in any way. She looked so calm, so beautiful. As though she understood. But how could that be?

"You just want to get on with it, do it on your own. You don't want to need anyone. Oh, Mack, we're more alike than you might think."

She leaned up and kissed his cheek. "Thank you for trusting me," she whispered. He was surprised to see her eyes mist over, but then she blinked and he wondered if he'd imagined it. He'd meant to tell her as a warning, that was all. A taste of what she was getting herself in for. Giving her the opportunity to back away now. Instead she turned the tables on him and was pleased he'd trusted her, when trust had little to do with it.

He was getting in deeper by the second.

"It occurs to me that we're both abysmal at holiday traditions." She sat up on her knees and reached for her bathrobe. "So here's what we're going to do. This place is completely devoid of holiday spirit. We're going to get a Christmas tree. Then we're going to go shopping and get decorations."

"Shopping?" He didn't attempt to hide the cynicism in his voice, but she continued undaunted.

"I don't even have a wreath or sprig of mistletoe." She dropped a peck on his lips and they fell open, amazed at this new, bubbly, tactile Kelley.

"The mall opens at noon," she chirped, tying the robe belt around her waist. "That leaves us this morning to find the perfect tree."

He raised his eyebrows. Silence hummed for a few seconds. This wasn't what he'd intended when he'd told her about his past. With one finger he reached over and tipped up her chin. "Maybe I want to spend the day with you. Just you. It's not often I take a day off this time of year, you know."

An adorable blush colored her cheeks. "So spend the day with me. We'll spend ridiculous amounts of money on Christmas kitsch. It'll be new."

She leaned over and kissed him, long and soft and sweet. "I want to do this for you, Mack. For both of us."

He couldn't resist her when she kissed him that way, full of promise and sweetness. He'd do it, but only for her. If she still believed a fairy-tale Christmas existed, he wouldn't be the one to play Scrooge.

"As long as you don't make me sing along with carols on the radio, fine. And when we come back I'll make you the best hot cocoa you've ever tasted." He ran a finger down the column of her throat. "Of course, it does mean you'll have to get dressed, and that's a bit of a shame."

"If we're going searching for a tree, we'd better get started." She blinked innocently.

"You," he said, pointing a finger and getting up off the bed, "are the devil to resist when you act like an angel." He kissed her forehead and then stopped at the bedroom door looking back over his shoulder. "How do you like your eggs?"

Her answer prompted a peal of laughter from him that lasted all the way down the stairs.

Mack tugged the toboggan behind him, making tracks that Kelley stepped in, following him to the edge of the pasture to the tree line. The cloud ceiling was high, and snowflakes fell around them, cocooning them in a shushing sound. For a few precious minutes, it was like they were the only two people in the world. The flakes floated to the ground, lying gently on the white blanket already there from the previous blizzard. He paused for a moment, and Kelley came up beside him, the clouds of their breaths mingling in the cold air. Fat snowflakes landed on her hat and stayed there, while her hazel eyes appeared even more green against the flush of her cheeks. He inhaled, his chest expanding, while the valley lay below them, Christmas-card perfect.

He was tugging a toboggan and carrying an ax to cut down a Christmas tree. It was inconceivable. He turned from the scene and began pulling again.

There had been an awkward moment when they'd gone to the main house to ask to borrow Jesse's sled to haul the tree back with. He'd said hello to Mrs. Hughes—who'd acted like nothing was out of the ordinary and insisted he call her Ruby. But Amelia had given him a speculative look he wasn't sure he'd liked. He'd felt under a microscope, as he had many times as a boy. Like he was being measured and found wanting.

"So who was this Boone guy, anyway?" Mack called back to Kelley, who was clumping along in her boots.

"Some guy who rescued Amelia and Jesse during the blizzard, and stayed on to work. But he's gone now."

"You didn't like him."

When the footsteps stopped behind him, he paused and looked over his shoulder. Kelley had stopped, her hands on her hips.

"I didn't trust him. That's all. He wasn't exactly truthful about his reasons for being here. He pretended to be the hand I'd hired on. And Amelia hasn't always shown the best judgment."

He bit his tongue. Guilt trickled through him. He hadn't been completely truthful with Kelley this morning, either. But he'd already revealed more than he had planned on telling a woman ever again.

Kelley had stopped, put her mittened hands into the pockets of her gray wool coat. A pink knitted hat covered her ears, but her blond curls cascaded over her shoulders. She looked like a winter angel.

"Maybe you should trust her more. We all made mistakes when we were younger."

"I'm just looking out for her. I'm her big sister. Jesse's father hurt her deeply. Am I wrong for not wanting that to happen again?"

"She's a big girl, Kelley. Old enough to know what she wants. Old enough to live with her own mistakes."

Kelley scowled. "That's more or less what she said."

He laughed, turned around and started pulling again. "So what would she say if she knew about you and me last night?"

He kept his back to her, kept pulling even though he would

like to have seen her face. After several more steps in silence, she answered.

"She does know. You were parked in my driveway all night. And she said be careful."

He stopped, dropping the cord to the toboggan and turned. She was only a step and a half away, her eyes gleaming in the brightness of reflected snow. There was a relief in not sneaking around.

"And are you? Careful?"

"It sure doesn't feel that way."

He took the extra step and put his gloved hands on her arms. "Then don't be careful for a little while longer, okay?" He wanted her this free, this unexpected, for a bit longer. Guileless and open. The holiday would be over soon and he didn't want to ruin it for her. Christmas Day was a day to be borne, that was all. Kelley was a balm against all of it.

He dipped his head and kissed her. She was soft and sweet and, yes, even innocent, despite what had transpired between them last night. "We can talk about her later," he murmured, his lips close to her cheek. "Right now, I've found you the perfect tree."

He stepped to the toboggan. He picked up the ax and made a well-aimed cut at the trunk of a fully rounded evergreen.

Kelley stood back and watched as Mack took swing after swing with the ax. A short week ago if someone had told her she'd be cutting a Christmas tree with Mack Dennison after a night of lovemaking, she would have laughed in their face. But here she was. She hadn't thought of him in terms as a lover. *Her lover.* And now whenever he was around, she felt the urge to girlify herself. For the first time ever, she felt feminine…and she liked it.

She wanted Mack for more than Christmas, and yet she wasn't sure how it could work. There'd been a brief idea that Boone would be staying on, and that would have been welcome help to Kelley, despite her reservations about his relationship with Amelia. But now…he was gone. She was tied to the Rocking H. And Mack was definitely tied to his business. She had to be realistic. She kept the thought around her like armor, even as she watched him, legs spread wide, shoulders flexing as he chopped down a perfectly shaped spruce tree. His breath made clouds as he struck the tree and exhaled. With a crack, the trunk gave and toppled over, a white cloud erupting in the snow as the branches splayed out.

She'd started out wanting to make Christmas for the family. Now that included Mack, too. What he'd told her this morning had been such a complete surprise. It was high time he had someone do something for him. It was unfamiliar territory, but one she thought they could enjoy discovering together.

Together they loaded the tree onto the sled and began the journey back to the house. Once back, Mack propped the tree up on the verandah and dusted off his hands. "Where's the stand?"

Kelley pulled off her mittens. "I don't have one."

"You don't?"

She smiled a little. "Don't act so surprised. We always celebrate at the main house. I guess we'll just have to get one in town today. Amelia already has a tree set up. She put it up for Jesse days ago."

"He's a cute kid."

Kelley grinned. "He is, isn't he? He made a wish for a daddy this year. I think being around other kids at school really made him see he was different."

Mack had a strange look on his face, a mix of pity and pain and withdrawal. Kelley wrinkled her brow. After what he'd told her this morning, she should have thought before opening her mouth.

"I didn't think…" she rushed to apologize.

He put his arm around her waist and gave a squeeze. "It's all right. I feel for the kid though. Knowing you're different is a hard thing to get used to. You look for ways to fit in. To hide it."

"Or you bury your nose in a book."

"Voice of experience?"

There was something in his voice that was almost defensive and she wondered at the strange turn of the conversation. "No more than yours. You must have found it so difficult."

"Kelley…"

She raised a hand. "I know. You don't want pity. You don't want to talk about it."

"No, I don't."

It wasn't so much what he said but what he didn't. His voice was completely flat, like he'd shut the door on something unpleasant. Kelley looked up at him, at once afraid and intrigued. She was curious, but to press might push him away and that was the last thing she wanted. Part of her wanted to hold his hand and help him as he'd helped her last night, even without knowing it. He had changed everything with his gentle touches and thorough loving. But another part begged her to leave it alone and not ruin this perfect day.

"Then let's go shopping. I'll spring for Candy Cane Fudge at the Creamery."

The dark cloud of his expression passed as she changed the subject. "That sounds good."

CHAPTER SEVEN

THE LAST OF THE PLASTIC packaging was in the garbage, the smell of cocoa came from the kitchen, and Kelley stood in the doorway to the living room, staring at her transformed house.

Evergreen boughs punctuated by red bows swooped from the loft railing, ending in a trail down the banister. A large bouquet of red poinsettias and white mums in a sleigh made a centerpiece on the pine coffee table. Cinnamon-scented candles glowed from a glass holder atop the mantel. A fired burned briskly in the fireplace, and their newly decorated tree stood proudly in the corner, a mass of twinkling lights and shining ornaments, a glorious white angel gracing the top. Kelley realized that for the first time ever, it looked like a home, not just a house. It was warm and welcoming.

In the kitchen Mack turned from the stove, whisk in hand, completing the festive picture. "Cocoa's nearly done."

Even in here she and Mack had worked magic. Now her table was dressed in a bright-red-and-green-plaid cloth. Green napkins were rolled and arranged in a glass jar, almost like a bouquet. It was all so pretty and perfect, like something out of a magazine.

"It smells wonderful. And the house looks gorgeous. Thank you, Mack, for doing all of this with me. I don't remember the last time I had so much fun..."

She stammered at the end, unsure of how to put her feelings so that he understood, and yet without frightening him away. There'd been times today he'd been so open, so relaxed. And then other times he'd seemed somehow distant, more like an observer than a participant. She knew which she preferred—how could she make him see it?

He turned off the burner and let the whisk sink into the creamy chocolate. His dark eyes touched on hers, and she wished he'd smile. If he smiled she could tell what he was thinking. Her heart pounded as he crossed the kitchen to where she was standing.

"I did it because I wanted to." He reached out and took one of her hands in his. "Being with you has been fun. I don't remember the last time I enjoyed Christmas. You did that, Kelley. Just you."

He paused, as if he was going to say something more, but the cell phone on his hip rang and he took it out of the holster. He looked at the number. "Do you mind?" he asked.

"No, go ahead." He'd been giving her a lot of his time lately; she understood he also had a business to run. She sipped the cocoa while he disappeared into the living room to talk. His business was in the city. Frequently traveling. And hers was here, at the Rocking H. With times getting tougher, she couldn't afford to hire more help. And she needed to keep the ranch profitable to sustain them all. It seemed unrealistic to be swept away in a flight of fancy. Perhaps they'd both been getting caught up in the magic of Christmas. Maybe she should just tuck the memories of last night away like a Christmas present, something special and surprising and unexpected.

"Did you see what else I bought?" His phone call finished, his smooth voice interrupted her thoughts and she bit her lip. He was smiling but there were new lines of strain around his eyes she hadn't seen before.

"No," she said weakly, and then he pointed up.

A sprig of mistletoe hung from the door frame, tied with a red ribbon.

She looked back down and into his eyes. And ceased caring about what would happen after Christmas Day or all the reasons why she should play it cautious. For once in her life she was going to get caught up in the moment. If ever there were a season for it, it was Christmas. She put her hand on his cheek before standing up on tiptoe and kissing him.

He put his hands on the small of her back and drew her closer as their mouths, tongues meshed. He tasted like mint and chocolate from their fudge earlier. His body was a hard, impenetrable wall as she pressed against it, absorbing its warmth and strength. If she got no other gift for Christmas, having Mack's arms around her was enough. He'd taken her fears of the physical and erased them with his first kiss. He'd made her feel wanted and hadn't run away at the first opportunity. He murmured into her mouth, and her pulse raced, fluttering frantically at her neck, wrist. This, just this, was enough.

"Mmmm," he murmured, pulling back so their lips parted. "Do you know how good you are at that?"

"Me?" She whispered it, their breaths mingling as they hovered at another kiss.

"Yeah, you," he replied.

She looked into his eyes, mesmerized by the tiny gold flecks around his pupils. "I haven't had much practice."

"If you improve, you're going to be the death of me, Miss Hughes." He grinned and a dimple appeared. "Come to think of it, maybe we'd better get started on your education. Practice does make perfect." And his mouth closed over hers again, slow and lingering.

A tiny bit of loneliness crept in even as her arms wrapped around his shoulders. What would happen after the holidays, when everything was put away? Would he disappear along with the bows and ribbons?

No. She refused to think of the new year and all the unknowns. She would not ruin it by thinking of things that hadn't even happened yet.

"As much as I would like to carry on this conversation upstairs, I have to go," he murmured, pressing a kiss to the tip of her nose. "Something's come up."

"Let it wait." She smiled up at him. "You deserve a day to yourself."

The lines around his eyes were back. "I wish," he murmured. "But I need to look after this."

"You could come back when you're done," she suggested. "We could watch a movie on TV."

His gaze fell to her mouth again, but then he exhaled. "I need some clean clothes. I wasn't actually expecting to spend the night last night."

Kelley had the silly urge to point out she had a washing machine. And a bathtub. The former he could use and the latter he could share, along with a healthy dose of bubbles. But the words stuck in her throat…they seemed so forward, so uncharacteristic of her. Not something she could blithely suggest or seduce her way into. It just wasn't in her. So she backed off, knowing that to feel she'd been rejected was foolish but feeling it just the same.

"That's okay. I'm sure having your truck parked out front two mornings in a row would raise some eyebrows at the house."

She turned away, pretending to tend the cocoa on the stove. She took a spoon and tried skimming off the thin skin that had formed on the top.

He came over and touched her hand, guiding it and helping scoop the skin on to a saucer. "You should be thankful your family cares."

"I am. But I have a right to my privacy."

"Not everyone has a family like yours, Kelley."

Her lips dropped open at his sharp tone. "I know that, too. Are we starting to argue? It feels like it and I don't know why."

"Don't you?"

The air hummed.

"No, I don't!" She grabbed the nearby ladle and started pouring the hot drink into mugs. She handed one to him. "Why don't you enlighten me?"

He put down his cup, reached over and took hers and put it down, too. Then he grabbed her upper arms and made her face him.

"You have a family that loves you. That cares for you and wants to protect you. You are moving heaven and earth to make Christmas for them, and I envy that."

Her eyes widened.

"This is the first Christmas I've spent any time with anyone other than a business associate. I've been in many cities around the world, but this is the first time I've cut down a tree and decorated it. Having a family whose opinion matters isn't something you take for granted!"

"I don't!"

"You've got everything here, don't you see that? And still you want more."

His censure stung, and she was done with apologizing for wanting something other than a solitary life on the family ranch. Something for herself. "I suppose you're an open book, right? There are parts of you, Mack Dennison, that are one big question mark."

He backed away as if her arms were suddenly scalding hot and burning his hands. "You don't know what you're talking about."

"I did hit a nerve." She felt herself getting angry now. He'd kissed her and held her and made love to her. He understood everything, and yet nothing. So much of him was a mystery.

"What you told me this morning hardly fills in all the blanks, Mack. And I don't know why you're suddenly so angry at me. You told me in the motel room that wanting more saved your life. I think I understand why you said that now. But why is it okay for *you* and not for *me?*"

"I didn't have what you have," he retorted.

"Your *last* store was the one you set up here, not your first. What were *you* running from?"

Mack decided to pick up his cocoa after all. He took one sip but it tasted bitter. He took the cocoa and dumped it down the sink.

He'd let himself get caught up in the Christmas fervor with her today. But that was just it. It was Christmas, a sentimental holiday illusion. In the bright light of the new year, everything would be much more clear. She was getting caught up in the holiday, that was all. It did funny things to people.

"I wasn't running from anything. I was building a life for myself."

"Then why did you come back?"

The answer was so close to the tip of his tongue it scared him. He'd had no choice. It was why the house on the bluff would now be his home.

Did she truly know what today had meant? What a leap it had been for a man like him? The last time he'd let himself need anyone was with Lissy, in London. He'd damn near bought her a ring. But the moment he'd told her the truth about his upbringing, the reason he was suddenly tied to Montana with invisible strings, he hadn't seemed nearly as attractive. He'd realized the links to his past were a liability. He'd spent that Christmas in a hotel in Los Angeles rather than in Lissy's London flat as planned. And he'd vowed he would never let himself need a woman again.

And as Kelley stared at him, he wanted to take away the hurt in her eyes and make her smile again. He was starting to seek her approval, wanting to please her, and the thought went a long way to cooling his heels.

"Let's just enjoy Christmas, okay? I don't want to argue with you. Not now."

He put a hand along her cheek, trying to soften her mutinous expression and failing. He had to get out of here now before he did something crazy, like tell her how he felt about her. He'd broken rules one and two, but three would stay in force. He couldn't be in love with her.

"I need to go now and look after this. I'll be back on Christmas Eve for final prep."

"That long." Her voice was like acid—he'd made her mad. Why did things have to get so complicated?

He laughed tightly, the sound thick with the undercurrents swirling in the room. "You've got everything you need in your fridge. Amelia's still doing dessert?"

"Yes, she is insistent she does the pies. It wouldn't be Christmas without her pies."

Another tradition he had no point of reference to. He felt as if walls were closing in and he had to get away. But he couldn't. He would go straight from here to the one place he dreaded more than any on earth.

"Right. I'll see you then."

Guilt crawled along his spine. And yet he couldn't bring himself to tell her the truth. He leaned over and kissed her forehead. "Bye, Kelley."

He left her standing there in the kitchen, with a mug full of cold cocoa and a little piece of his heart left behind.

Christmas Eve dawned as all Christmas Eves should: cheerfully bright, white and crisp. When Kelley got out of bed, it was with a sense of excitement she hadn't had since she'd been a small child. Today Mack was coming back. She'd fix what had gone wrong between them. It was Christmas Eve! Anything was possible.

Today they were going to make ahead the orange salad and cranberry sauce. They would forget their harsh words and focus on having a merry Christmas.

She touched a finger to an angel ornament, remembering what he'd said when he'd bought it for her. That it reminded him of her. All she knew was that she wasn't ready for it to be over after tonight. She needed him to know how much he meant to her. And that meant sharing with him, too.

She showered and dressed carefully, in low-slung jeans and a soft sweater than hugged her slim form more than she was used to. She pulled a small amount of hair back from each side of her face, holding it with a small clip, while the rest of her hair fell down her back. The interest in her appearance was a first. She realized that with Mack she didn't want to hide. She wanted him to see her. And she wanted him to like what he saw.

She pressed a hand to her nervous tummy as he arrived, carrying a bag with the fresh ingredients required for the day. "Good morning." He smiled, pushing his boots off with his toes and handing her the groceries, as if their harsh words had never happened. "And Merry Christmas."

The bubbles of excitement fizzed stronger as he dropped a light kiss on her lips. More than ever she was determined to prove to him that she could do this. That his faith in her hadn't been misplaced. But more than that, she wanted to show him how things could be between them. Not just today. Every day.

"Are you ready for your next lesson?"

"I put myself in the hands of the master."

"Well now. That's a dangerous spot to be in." He winked at her and she laughed. Perhaps she'd just imagined his darker mood of Sunday afternoon, for right now it was lighter than it had been all week. More than ever she wanted to tell him everything—about how he'd changed things for her, about how she wanted more time with him. It was a matter of waiting for the right moment. Maybe tonight, when it was just the two of them in front of the tree…

"A dangerous spot for you," she joked. "I know you. You won't be able to keep your hands off my turkey."

She put the bag on the counter, thrilled when his arms snaked around her waist. "I won't be able to keep my hands off something," he agreed.

Kelley turned within the circle of his arms and looked up. He was smiling and teasing but there was something else lurking behind his eyes. She wished she knew what it was. "You're different today."

His arms tightened and his gaze dropped to her lips before moving back up. "I missed you, Kel."

"I missed you, too." Her heartbeat quickened as he dropped a light kiss on her lips, then another. It was the closest he'd gotten to an admission of his feelings. But was it enough? Could they make it work beyond Christmas? She knew she wanted it to.

Mack's heart swelled at her words and he kissed her because he didn't know what to say. He had missed her. And in missing her, he'd discovered something very unpleasant. He needed her. And he didn't like needing anyone. He had to find a way to let her go, for both their sakes. But not today. He wasn't so cruel that he'd do it today.

He touched her nose with a finger. "Today is Christmas Eve. The final countdown to your culinary triumph. Should we get started? If we finish early…"

When everything was ready, Kelley wiped the last dish, looked around the kitchen with the cranberry sauce a ruby-red ribbon in a glass dish, the orange salad arranged prettily on a snowflake-patterned plate. Tomorrow she'd prepare vegetables and turkey at the main house, and they'd all sit down to a holiday meal together. With one extra. She smiled to herself. The phone call from Boone today had been a surprise. It was all going to work out—for all of them. She just knew it.

"Well, let's hope the execution goes as well as the preparation," she said, standing back and brushing her hands down her apron. She untied it from around her waist and hung it over a chair. "Thank you, Mack. For everything. When I walked into your store…"

"I know," he replied. He stood in front of the counter, his hands in his pockets. The afternoon sun bathed him in light through the window above the sink. "I didn't expect you. I sure didn't expect any of this to happen."

How could she ever get through dinner, when she was dying inside, longing to tell him how she felt? She swallowed and gathered up some courage. "I was scared to death. I had to be to ask for help, you realize that, right? But I don't regret it, not for a moment. I hope you don't, either."

He came over to her then, and framed her face with his hands. "Kelley the Stubborn. So determined." His smile was soft. "Is that what you think? That I regret it?"

She couldn't answer, so she shrugged.

"Making love to you had been on my mind for days. Ever since the night in the motel room. Maybe even before then…maybe as far back as seeing you walk into my store, pretending to know what you were about."

She laughed, a soft, almost-sob. A sentimental Mack was a treat she hadn't expected. "I had no idea."

"I'm not sorry for anything that's happened the last week. Not one thing."

She took a deep breath and tilted her chin so she could look up at him. It was a sweet thing to say, so why did she get the feeling it was a first step to goodbye?

She rested her fingers on the waistband of his jeans. "That being the case…I was going to ask you. Do you want to stay tonight?"

She held her breath. *Please say yes*. She wanted to share Christmas with him. All of it. She'd never had a significant other to share holidays with, and it was so much more cozy with two. She wanted his face to be the first one she saw as dawn crept over the white hills. To know that she wasn't alone. To watch him over the rim of a coffee cup with the lit tree behind them. Simple things, but special ones.

"I'd love to, but I'm due at the shelter, remember?" There was a trace of regret in his voice. She grabbed on to it.

"Come back when you're done. I'll leave the tree on and a fire burning."

"Why do you want me to, Kelley?"

"Because…because…" She stammered for a few moments. Why did she want him there? And it wasn't just about the sentimentality of the holiday, or not wanting to be alone. She knew that. It went deeper. So much deeper she could hardly breathe. The words sat on her tongue while she deliberated if she should say them or not. The differences between them, the secrets, vanished when he was like this with her. All that mattered was the way he touched her, spoke to her. And if she didn't say it now, she might not have another chance.

"Because Christmas is meant to be spent with people you love." Her words came out on a quiet whisper, yet they echoed to every corner of the room. "Don't you think, Mack?"

He backed away. "Kelley…"

"You have to know what this week has meant to me. And I need to tell you, Mack, because being with you, it changed *everything*. More than you can imagine."

She sighed, knowing she wanted to do this but finding it unbearably difficult just the same. "I don't think you realize how much," she murmured. Her eyes captured his. "I need to tell you something, Mack, so you'll understand. But please…I need your arms around me when I do."

He hesitated a moment, but then took a step forward, holding out his hands. "Come here," he whispered, and she went into the safe circle of his arms.

He was warm and strong and all those things that had made her trust him in the first place. When she'd gathered strength from his embrace, she pulled back just a little. Close enough to feel the heat from his body, far enough away that she could have the room to speak.

The kitchen smelled of spices and cranberries. Kelley knew

she would succeed in making a beautiful family dinner. It had been her goal, and yet it all seemed silly and trivial at this moment. His gaze darkened, held reservations, but she expected that. She felt as though she were standing on the edge of something, and one small slip could ruin it all.

She reached up with trembling fingers and touched his cheek. "Being with you the other night changed something in me. I didn't think I'd ever be able to unfreeze enough to be with a man, Mack. But with you it was different. I saw you with Risky and I wondered if you were the one who would be gentle enough, understanding enough. And you were."

"I don't understand."

"When you told me about your childhood, I knew you'd understand. Oh, Mack, you're not the only one with secrets. I've never told anyone about this. Not Gram, not Amelia…but I want you to know, Mack."

She gripped his hands, a lifeline to get her through it. She'd never once said the words out loud, not even to herself.

"I know you felt unloved and unwanted by your mum. But you're not, not by me. I want you to know how much you've given me. The truth is, when we graduated…"

Her throat closed over as images raced through her mind, followed by crippling fear. She could almost feel his hands again, hear the raspy sound of his mocking voice. Her breath quickened and she closed her eyes.

No. It was over and done. Wilcox had left Rebel Ridge a long time ago, and he no longer held any power over her. She replaced the images with the memory of lying in Mack's arms, feeling loved and cherished. Two solitary tears gathered at the corners of her eyes and squeezed out, rolling silently down her cheeks.

"Kelley." His voice was a hushed whisper, his fingers firm on hers. Reassuring.

"The truth is, on prom night I was raped, and I haven't been with a man since. Until you."

CHAPTER EIGHT

THE WORDS SENT A RUSH of relief flooding through Kelley's body. Saying them out loud was cathartic. Suddenly they didn't have the same power. Being with Mack had made it possible to move on. Just saying the words opened up new vistas for her. She wanted to see places, experience things. No more hiding away.

"What?" Mack's voice was filled with disbelief, and he stepped back, leaving her without the shelter of his arms. She shivered, feeling the sudden cold. She'd thought the hard part was over, but the euphoric release only lasted a minute. Explaining was going to be much more difficult than she imagined.

"It happened after the prom," she began, her voice wobbling a little. "I…I had a date for the dance, and I thought I was ready. So many of the other girls…and he was popular and handsome…looking back now I think I just wanted to feel feminine, and pretty, and wanted. Gram had taken me to buy a new dress and it was so beautiful."

She started to choke on the words and fought to regain control. "I was always the tomboy, you see."

"You hid behind boots and jackets and braids."

She nodded, relieved he understood. "When he asked me out, I went. I didn't know I was being used. But at the last minute…I changed my mind. But he didn't care. We weren't at the party everyone had gone to. Instead we went to a cabin out back of their spread. It was small and dark and I heard the click of the door locking. I...I can still hear it in my nightmares. I asked to leave but then he grabbed me and..."

Her lips quivered uncontrollably now as tears swelled over her bottom lashes. She could still feel the hands that had seemed to be everywhere at once, and her stomach churned. "I should have fought him off, right?" Her voice sounded small and far away. "I didn't fight him and I should have."

"He raped you." The words came out dull, dead. Final.

She shrugged pitifully. "I said no, but he didn't like that. In the end...oh, Mack," she pleaded. "In the end... It was horrible and heartbreaking. Even now, I hate being in dark places. The motel room during the blizzard was awful."

Mack stared at her, tears staining her cheeks and her lips quivering. Never had he expected this. He'd known she was innocent; not a virgin obviously, but her sweetness had said it all. But dammit, what was he supposed to do with *this?* The magnitude of it all crashed down on Mack and he had no idea what to say, how to act. If only she'd said something. Dear Lord, he'd kissed her in that room, sensed she was nervous, but had never imagined something like this. If he'd known, he would never have left her to sit through the storm all alone.

"I'm not sure how...I mean...why me?"

She sent him a tenuous smile. "You're wonderful, that's why. Being with you was...a revelation. I wasn't afraid. I trusted you. I knew after seeing you with Risky that you'd be gentle and kind and..."

Suddenly she broke off and her face flamed.

The magnitude sunk in and Mack knew exactly what he'd done. He'd gone and seduced a woman completely unprepared for it. It hadn't been a level playing field. And he'd stupidly told himself he was in control, but the truth was, *he'd* needed *her.* And he'd taken her without any thought as to what effect it would have. He rubbed a hand over his face.

That made him a selfish bastard. Careless. He'd ignored the signs. The way she'd been timid, innocent, the way she'd been afraid in the motel room...he'd thought only of himself.

Because he needed her.

And it scared him to death.

"Why now? Why tell me now?"

Tears glimmered on her cheeks and he felt about two inches tall.

"Because I fell in love with you. Because you trusted me and I thought I could trust you."

His breath came out in a whoosh. How could he possibly tell her that he'd only talked about his childhood in an effort to put distance between them? And that it had the opposite effect? He paced to the tree, staring at the lights that all seemed to blur together.

He felt as though he was drowning and needed a life preserver. All he could think about was how she must have been terrified. Thinking about another man's—no, boy's—hands on her skin when she'd said no. It damn near broke his heart. What must it have taken for her to let him...knowing what had come before...

He hung his head, letting out a raw breath. There were things she didn't know. She'd been through enough. How could he possibly burden her any further with his own problems? They certainly weren't going away. She was just embarking on her life, making all these self-discoveries. And he was the one tied down.

"You said love," he whispered hoarsely. "Love is a word that gets thrown around far too often, and when it's convenient."

Her eyes took on a wounded look. "You don't believe me."

He had to turn away. He'd had no agenda. He'd said he'd help her. He'd agreed to let her hire him. He'd even trusted her with the story of his mother. How had it ever come to this?

She was really crying now and it killed him to see her red-rimmed eyes. He'd trusted her. He needed her. He'd fallen in love with her. All three rules broken. It was a complete disaster. She deserved better than him. She was ready to spread her wings. He would only slow her down.

"I can't do this," he said, swallowing thickly against the knot of denial. "There are things..." He stopped just short of saying the words. His jaw tightened. "You don't need me, Kelley. You need someone who can put you first."

"And you can't?"

He closed his eyes. What got him most was that he wanted to believe her, and knowing it caused that slow, sick turning he recognized as dying hope. Just like he'd wanted to believe the others. Like he'd believed his mother every time a promise had been made. Like he'd believed Lissy when she'd said the words. But at the end of the day, none of them stayed.

And then a cowgirl in crisis had shown up at his shop and turned everything upside down. And he knew that to let himself hope with her was different. He'd given her his heart without even realizing it. And if he told her, and then lost her...he was pretty damn sure this time he wouldn't bounce back.

He heard her sniff and was filled with self-loathing. She only thought she felt this way. In time she'd realize he wasn't right for her. And yet somehow the little boy inside still longed to hear the words.

"What do you want, Kelley?" He said the words slowly, testing them out. "Because it's more than a turkey and a Christmas tree. What do you see happening between us?"

Kelley gathered what little bit of courage she had left around her. This wasn't how she'd planned it to go. She'd wanted his arms around her, comforting words of love and support. She'd wanted to tell him how she felt, and she'd hoped he would feel the same way. Instead she was faced with a cold stranger, and she did the only thing she knew how to do. She couldn't let herself fall apart again, even though she was quaking on the edge of it. She'd come too far.

She tried to cover her hurt with ice. "If you think I asked you to stay out of some misplaced obligation, you're perfectly mistaken. I asked you because I thought we shared something special, and that you might want to share your first 'real' Christmas with me."

"If it's because of what I told you and..."

She couldn't let him finish. She had to press forward. "Did you think what we shared was part of your payment? Or that I did it out of what, misplaced pity? Or worse, that I *used* you?" This wasn't about hiring him, or feeling sorry for a poor misused boy. It was because of the man he'd become. Why couldn't he see that?

At his lack of response, she tilted her chin. "I thought you thought more of me than that. I thought you saw me for *me*."

"I do," he uttered, his deep voice hoarse as he stood before the tree they'd decorated together. "Believe me, Kelley, your feelings now aren't real. One day you'll turn around and I'll just be 'that guy' that helped you get over 'that time.'"

"Do you really think so little of me?" Her mouth dropped open in dismay. "Of yourself?"

"No! And…" He paused. Sighed. "This was never part of the plan. And now you tell me you were…raped…" He seemed to struggle over the word. "And I feel like someone sucker punched me."

His eyes darkened with anguish. "I can't get past the picture of his hands on you." He took a shuddering breath. "I'm angry…and I'm feeling helpless. And those are two emotions I've had to work very hard to overcome."

It was becoming clear he couldn't handle the truth. She'd been a fool to think he could. This was exactly why she hadn't told him before. "Are you saying you don't want to see me again?"

"I got caught up in the moment with you. I wanted a real Christmas and I fell for it all. But that's not what's real. Life isn't this way every day—all perfect and pretty and goodwill toward men. Sometimes it's ugly and lonely."

"You are a coward."

The words came out of her mouth in an impulsive, hurtful rush, and Mack recoiled against the blow. It was as though she'd driven a knife between his ribs, cutting off his air. He'd wanted desperately to be wrong. For her to tell him he'd been wrong. But he deserved it. Every single bit. He could turn it around and around all he wanted, use her eleventh-hour revelation as an excuse, but the truth was he would only hurt her, and ending it now would be doing her a favor. He couldn't ask her to take him on. Not with everything he had to deal with these days.

"You're right. I am a coward."

Her eyes glittered as her back straightened. There was none of the timidity, none of the self-consciousness he'd seen. In its place was a strength that was beautiful to behold, even as her words of truth cut into him like knives.

"You, Mack, are lying to yourself. So what if you helped me move past what was holding me back? That doesn't mean it was meaningless." She went to him and touched his arm. He looked down at her fingers but resisted the urge to cover them with his own. Something was happening here, something bigger than asking him to spend Christmas. Something he couldn't face.

"Kelley," he began, but she cut him off.

"In fact, I think the only reason it did work was because it *wasn't* meaningless. I believe in my heart it could only have been with *you*. And if knowing it makes you scared, well join the club. It frightens the hell out of me. I'll be damned if I'll run away from it. You made me love you. But you go ahead and be a coward."

She went to her purse and took out a check. "Here you go. Paid in full. Just like we agreed."

She opened his palm and put the paper in it, then closed his fingers over top. She turned away and disappeared into the kitchen.

For a few moments he thought about going after her. But then he remembered the phone call on Sunday, knew where he'd be tomorrow afternoon. This was for the best. He quietly put on his things, tucking the check back into her purse as he went out the door.

Kelley sat at the kitchen table, her hands folded in front of her. He hadn't come back. Hadn't called. She missed him. All week she'd imagined having him beside her tonight. She'd imagined giving him the tiny present she'd picked up on impulse as they sat next to the tree. She had wanted to put on the new dress she'd bought and fix her hair and feel beautiful.

Instead, she'd had a good cry, and then gone upstairs and changed into a pair of soft pyjamas. Tomorrow she'd put on a merry face and do the family Christmas.

For tonight she was just miserable.

She got up and made a pot of coffee. The familiar smell of Mack's special grind reminded her of the morning she'd awakened with him sitting on the side of the bed. She missed him with a loneliness so unfamiliar and sharp that she had a hard time breathing. Now Boone was coming back, and Amelia was going to have her chance at happiness. Kelley had thought it was going to work out for all of them. And while she was happy for her sister, it was a stark reminder of how she'd come so close and lost.

She took her coffee and turned on the television. It was all Christmas programming—the day simply could not be ignored. She left it on *White Christmas,* but only half paid attention to Bing Crosby and Rosemary Clooney crooning at each other. She thought of Mack, earlier tonight, serving dinner to the homeless. Why hadn't she volunteered to go with him when he'd first told her? Would it have made a difference in the end?

In a matter of minutes it would be Christmas Day. And despite all her planning, she was alone.

The lights on the tree glittered, reflecting off the foil-wrapped gift that lay beneath the branches. Inside was a set of ornaments in the shape of kitchen utensils. She'd hoped that tonight they could put them on the tree together. Kneeling down, she picked up the box and ran her hand over the paper, feeling the awful urge to cry. She'd come out from beneath the heavy mantle of her hurts, but he hadn't. Her heart ached for the boy who had been so lonely. A man who wouldn't—couldn't—trust.

A man who didn't love her. Who would rather leave than let himself give in to love—to being loved.

The knock on the door startled her out of her musings. She pressed a hand to her heart, her first thought that it might be Mack. She stood upright and let out a breath, surprised that the hope hit her so hard. It was probably just Amelia with some last-minute thought about tomorrow's dinner.

She opened the door and there he was.

His breath made a cloud in the bitter night as a few flakes of snow fluttered beyond the verandah. His hands were in his jacket pockets, the sheepskin collar turned up against the cold.

The frigid air sneaked into the house through the open door as seconds passed.

"I missed you," he said finally.

A tiny glimmer of hope kindled. He was here. She wouldn't risk him leaving again; tonight there could be nothing but absolute truth.

"I missed you, too."

"And I want to be with you," he said, his dark eyes holding hers captive. "I love you, Kelley."

The glimmer burst into flame as he stepped forward, surrounded her with his arms, kicking the door shut behind him. For the moment nothing else mattered...she was in his arms again. He was there, for her. Everything else melted away.

"I love you, too, Mack."

He put her down, cradled her cheekbones with his thumbs. "You mean it? Even after everything I said today?"

"Yes, I do."

He dipped his head and touched his lips to hers, gently, reverently. "I'm sorry about this afternoon," he whispered, dotting light kisses on her cheeks. "Nothing came out right."

She put her arms around him and rested her head on his wide shoulder. The fabric of his coat was still cold from outside, and she inhaled the leathery scent of winter mixed with the clean cologne she now knew was simply Mack. "Keep going," she said softly. "You're doing okay so far."

He laughed, a low, sexy rumble that somehow turned the world right again. "Look at you," he marveled, standing back and holding her hands out.

She belatedly realized she was in cream-colored flannel pyjamas, and that she'd done nothing with her hair since taking it out of the clip. "Oh, don't look at me! I'm a mess!"

"You're beautiful. All cream and pink and...your hair is down." He let go of her hands and reached out, touching a golden strand. "I love it when your hair is down."

Tears stung her eyelids. "Thank you."

Kelley closed her eyes. He was here. Really here. "I missed you so much. I didn't think you were coming back."

"I didn't, either. Until I realized I wanted to stop running." He led her to the sofa and they sat down. "I've been running for so long I'm not sure I know how to do anything else."

She squeezed his hand. "That's a start."

"Why did you come to *me?*" he said at last. "Why did you ask me for help?"

"I think I was just meant to be there, at that time, in that place. And there you were. The answer to all my problems, and I didn't even know it."

He nodded slowly. Kelley watched him struggle with something, and her heart softened even more. "What about you, then? Why did you agree?"

"I saw you were trying to give. To give something of yourself to make it easier for the family you obviously love. I never had a Christmas with decorated trees or dinners or presents. I never saw one where a family loved each other enough to go the extra mile. What you were doing—it was selfless."

He looked down at their fingers. "You were like that with me, too. And I pushed you away. You deserve better than me," he whispered hoarsely. "You deserve more than the kid of an alcoholic who couldn't have cared less whether her son lived or died, a child who didn't matter."

"You can't turn back the clock. You can't pretend it didn't happen. You do matter. To so many people. To me. Oh, Mack, I know." Her lip quivered but she pressed on, knowing he had to understand exactly how she felt. "You know why Mack's Kitchen works for you? Because you can still be on the outside looking in. And as scary as that is, it's not nearly as scary as dealing with it. Just like me being with a man was too frightening to think about. Until you. You took my fears away."

Mack turned away first, faced the Christmas tree. She was right; he knew it.

"You give other people what you want for yourself, but are too afraid to believe in." She rubbed a hand between his shoulder blades as he nodded. He could feel the warmth even through his heavy coat. He'd gone to the shelter this afternoon, still angry and confused. But as he'd served a turkey dinner to those without homes, his thoughts were always with Kelley. The pleasure he normally felt in helping out was soured. And he'd realized in a very painful way that the rest of his life was destined to be the same if he didn't stop tap-dancing around the facts and just be honest. He needed her. And it was okay.

"When I was home alone tonight I realized that the work was just a substitute for happiness. I went to the shelter, but the joy of helping was gone from it. Because you are my joy. I had you and I lost you."

He looked into her eyes. They were so beautiful, hazel with the green flecks reflected by the mellow glow from the tree. "And then a couple came in. They had nothing. Their clothes were threadbare, their faces wrinkled. But they were holding hands. Her hands were so shaky." He swallowed as he recalled the way the woman's fingers had trembled as she'd reached for her plate.

"They took their dinner and sat together and he reached over and buttered her roll. Such a small gesture, but she smiled at me and I knew. He will always be there for her, no matter what. It's you, Kelley. It's you I need." He leaned forward, squeezed her hand as he emphasized, *"Just you."*

"Oh, Mack…"

"I was afraid. Afraid to trust in you, believe in you. But more than that…I was afraid to believe in myself. I set up those walls to protect myself because loving you made me vulnerable. Only, it doesn't work without you."

But there was more he needed to say, to explain. He should have been truthful with her all along. He should have trusted her the way she'd trusted him. "So now I have to be completely honest."

He paused, tempted to stare at his hands but knowing he had to face this dead on. He had to trust her. They'd come this far. "Tomorrow at the rehab center…" He swallowed. He could do this. "It's not just volunteering. I go to see my mother."

Kelley gasped, her eyes darting to his. Of all the things he could have said, he knew she hadn't expected this, and guilt snaked through him once more.

"Don't look at me that way," he said. "I know I should have told you."

"I thought you didn't know where your mother was."

"I didn't want to have to explain." He ran his hands through his hair. "And her body *is* there, Kel, but it's broken. And I don't know where her mind is. She left after high school, but I never heard from her again. Until I got a call that she was in hospital, and she'd listed me as her next of kin. She'd been drinking. She'd had an accident. The damage was permanent. She can't tell me from one of the orderlies."

She reached out and covered his hand with hers. "Oh, Mack. How horrible. For both of you."

He blinked against the compassion in her voice. "It's why I finally came back, you know. At least this way I can be closer to her. Someone has to pay her bills. I don't want her in some dingy room without a window."

"I'm so sorry. I can only imagine that growing up, you must have wished for things to change. And that with her accident…"

"Yes. There's no chance of it now. Maybe I should hate her for my childhood, but…"

"But she's your mother." She smiled softly, rubbing her thumb over the top of his hand. "And you still care about her and want to look after her."

He nodded, fighting back emotion. She understood. He wished he'd trusted her enough in the beginning to tell her. "The phone call the other day—that was the nurse on duty. My mother asked for me. That's the first time it's happened since the accident. But by the time I got there, she was gone again. And I was angry. I had let myself hope again."

"Of course you did." Kelley smiled. "A part of you always wanted to believe."

His fingers squeezed hers. "The last woman I told was two years ago. Our relationship ended very abruptly. I was afraid to tell anyone again, afraid to care so much about someone that it mattered."

"What changed your mind?"

He raised his hand and ran it down her hair. The tree lights glimmered off it. She was his angel, he realized. His everyday angel. Not just one for Christmas Eve or bringing out on holidays. She was the kind of woman who was strong enough to be there day in and day out. He twisted a few strands of her hair between his fingers. "You."

"Me?"

He smiled into her surprised face. "Yes, you. The weight's

heavy, Kelley. And I realized that you had put your faith in me when you told me about your rape. And if you were willing to trust me with something so painful, then I could trust you. I just needed to admit it to myself."

Kelley looked down at their joined hands. It was like a world opened up to her, one with more colors and facets than she even knew existed. "You don't have to go through it alone, Mack."

His breath came out with a whoosh as he pulled her close. "I spent a lot of Christmases all over the world looking for a miracle," he said into her hair. "And it was right here all along."

Tears clogged her throat as her fingers dug into his back. "Right back at you," she whispered. And when she finally eased her grip on him, he kissed her. Again, and again, and once more, as if he was afraid she would disappear from his embrace.

She got up from the sofa and went to the tree, picking up the present she'd bought for him. "Here," she said, holding it out. "It's not much. But when I saw it…"

He undid the ribbon and wrapping, grinning at the display of miniature utensils inside. "For your tree."

"For our tree," she corrected. He stood, handed her a tiny potato masher sporting holly on the handle and tied with gold ribbon. "Here. You should hang the first one."

Together they hung the ornaments and stood back to admire.

"I realized something tonight," she whispered, leaning back into the shelter of his arms. The fire had burned down, leaving only glowing embers. "The truth is I've hidden behind this ranch for so long I don't think I realized I was even doing it. It was my one thing, you know. And I held on to it tight."

"And now you're letting go?"

"I didn't put enough faith in people, either. Amelia deserved more of it. And now…well, her happy ending is on his way here. Things are going to change around the Rocking H. I don't have to hold on to it with both hands."

"You're giving up the ranch?"

She laughed. "Not completely. Maybe I can hang on with one hand?" She leaned back so she could look up at him. "And hang on to someone else with the other?"

"I like that idea. As long as I'm the someone else."

"You don't see any other sexy chefs around here, do you?"

He laughed. "There'd better not be. In any case, I'm glad to hear it. Because I was kind of hoping that I could pull you away for a few days."

She smiled then, a soft smile filled with sweetness. "Where are we going?"

"How does Washington sound? I have a short trip there for work in the new year. It's not very glamorous…but it is convenient."

She slid closer to him, felt his arm tighten her, warm and secure. "It works for me. As long as you're there."

"And after that…I'll take you anywhere you want to go. London. Paris. Rome."

The idea was so big she could barely comprehend it. But while she'd always felt the need to see things, there was something that suddenly mattered more.

"I got you something, too," he said casually.

"You did?"

He went over to his jacket and fumbled in the pocket. When he came back, he held up a sprig of mistletoe.

"It worked once before…"

She stepped forward and placed her hands on his chest. "Powerful stuff, that mistletoe." And she kissed him as he held the mistletoe above their heads.

When she stepped back, breathless, he smiled, like he had a secret.

"What?"

"It worked. Mistletoe is supposed to be a plant of truce. Even among lovers."

"You didn't think you needed reinforcements, did you? Not that I'm complaining."

"Now, about that travel. Paris. London. Rome," he continued thoughtfully, "any of those places would be wonderful for a honeymoon."

She put a hand to her chest. "A honeymoon!"

"Yes, a honeymoon." He lowered the mistletoe and she saw something dangling from the center of the clump. "Oh…"

It was a ring. Not a traditional engagement ring encrusted

with diamonds, but a wide white-gold band with an inlaid filigree design. Tiny diamonds winked from within the setting. She couldn't have picked anything more beautiful herself.

"I left the shelter and saw it in the store window. They were just closing up, but when I explained…" He unfasted the ring from its anchor. "I thought it would suit you for everyday, even when you were working. I didn't want to get you a ring you could only wear on special occasions." He slid it off the ribbon and poised it at the tip of her finger. "An everyday ring, for my everyday miracle."

She blinked rapidly as he looked down at her, so earnest, his dark eyes so full of love. For her.

"Will you marry me, Kelley? We can live here if you want…. I know you like being close to your family. Although, the house is almost done and would be much bigger for our family…if you want babies. But it's your choice."

The tears that clogged her throat earlier returned, making it impossible to speak. After a life of always doing what was expected, to be given a choice was glorious. The horizons were bright and wide. And Mack would be beside her.

"Yes." She found her voice. "Yes, I will marry you. And we can live anywhere as long as we can fill it with babies. If that's what *you* want."

"I want," he confirmed.

The clock chimed the hour and she sighed. "Merry Christmas, Mack."

"Merry Christmas, sweetheart."

EPILOGUE

KELLEY CARRIED THE TURKEY to the table on Great-Grandma Hughes's ivory platter. Dishes glittered on the pristine white tablecloth. On a side table a tray of asparagus puffs was down to crumbs, and the bottle of champagne Mack had brought was nearly empty. She caught Mack's gaze as he talked with Boone; his eyes twinkled back at her. Jesse knelt on the floor with his new train set while Gram sat in her rocker, overseeing the locomotive's progress on the track. Amelia helped bring out the last of the dishes and for a moment the two sisters looked over their family.

"It's a picture, isn't it?" Kelley spoke softly, looking at her sister's beaming face. She smoothed the red-and-green apron that was protecting her new dress. "Everyone together. Gram hale and hearty, Jesse so happy. And you, too. I'm so happy for you, sis." She reached down and squeezed Amelia's hand.

"It worked out," her sister said simply, but the smile that had been on her face since this morning had yet to fade. "And you look beautiful. A dress, and makeup. And did you blow dry your hair?"

Kelley felt a blush rise to her cheeks. She had put in extra effort this morning. It was an important morning. And she and Mack had decided together to wait for the right time to share their news.

"Let's call them all to the table," Kelley suggested, and left the task to Amelia, watching as her sister rounded up the family with motherly efficiency. She swallowed against the emotion rising in her throat. To think that such a short time ago, things had been so different. Now Boone was here and they were going to join forces with the neighboring ranch he'd bought. As they all took their places around the table, Kelley slid the ring out of her apron pocket and back onto her finger, where it belonged.

"Gram? Will you do the honors?"

Ruby's voice rang out, strong and clear as she gave the simple but heartfelt blessing. "Lord, thank you for this blessed holiday, for health, happiness and bringing all of us together. Amen."

Kelley cleared her throat as the five bowed heads raised. "Well…" She gave a little laugh. "Before our professional carves the turkey, I have an announcement to make."

She got to her feet, feeling five other pairs of eyes on her. "First, my big sister welcome-to-the-family to Boone. I've never seen Jesse so happy or my sister so radiant." Boone and Amelia smiled at each other, and Kelley felt the warmth of their love clear to her toes. "I was pretty happy to hear you were on your way back to these parts, Gifford. Welcome home."

Boone stood and came around the table to give her a hug. As he did, her ring sparkled on her left hand and Amelia gave a gasp.

"Kelley?"

She stepped back from Boone's embrace and reached down to her right to take Mack's hand.

"Oh, yes, I nearly forgot!" She laughed, knowing something so wonderful could never have slipped her mind. She gazed down into Mack's eyes. She would never tire of seeing that look there, just for her. "Mack proposed last night and I accepted."

There was a general scrape of chairs against floor as they were pushed back, squeals of excitement and congratulations echoing through the room. Amelia rushed forward to hug her sister, Boone and Mack shook hands, and Gram came forward to give each and every one of them a hug while she dabbed at her eyes with a red-and-white handkerchief. "It's about time we had some menfolk around here," she announced.

When the hubbub quieted, Mack presided over the turkey, while bowls were passed and plates filled. Everything had turned out just right. Kelley had cooked a beautiful dinner with only the slightest input from Mack, who seemed reluctant to let her out of his sight. As Kelley ate, she listened to the chatter around her…two more places set this year, twice the happiness. What would next year bring?

But Jesse was being unusually quiet and she wrinkled her brow. He'd wanted a father so desperately. What could be wrong?

"Jesse?"

"Yes, Aunt Kelley?"

"You okay, sweetheart? You're awfully quiet."

He shrugged. "Just thinkin'."

She hid a smile behind her finger. "Thinkin' about what?"

Forks paused as everyone seemed interested in his answer.

"Well," he said, thoughtfully scooping up a helping of potato, "I was just wondering. Does this mean I'm gonna have a daddy *and* an uncle, too?"

Her hand slid away from her mouth and she couldn't hold back the smile at the innocent question.

"Yes, Jesse, that's exactly what it means. Is that okay?"

His eyes widened, a gorgeous picture of boyish wonderment. "Oh, yeah, it's okay."

He leaned over and tugged at Ruby's sleeve. "Hey, Grandma?" he whispered, just loudly enough so everyone could hear.

"Yes, Jesse?"

"You were right, Grandma. About Santa."

Kelley's eyes stung with happy tears as she laughed. It was as though a little miracle had suddenly happened right here at the Rocking H. And as she took Mack's hand under the table, she understood that sometimes all you really needed to do was just believe.

* * * * *

This season we bring you
Christmas Treats
For an early Christmas present Donna Alward would like to share a little treat with you....

MACK DENNISON'S ASPARAGUS PUFFS

6 tbsp/85g butter
12 asparagus spears
12 sheets phyllo pastry
1½ cup/120g Parmesan cheese
12 thin slices of prosciutto ham
Mack's Kitchen dill seasoning*

Preheat the oven to 450°F/230°C

Trim the root ends off the asparagus. On a cutting board, spread out one sheet of phyllo, keeping the remaining sheets under a damp cloth. Using a pastry brush, brush the sheet with butter and fold it over on itself. Sprinkle the surface with dill seasoning and Parmesan.

Lay a slice of ham on top, then an asparagus spear, and roll up. Brush with butter and cut into 2-inch/5-cm lengths. Lay on a nonstick baking sheet. Repeat with the remainder of the ingredients. Bake for 10 minutes until golden brown. May be served hot or cold!

*To make dill seasoning: Mix 2 tbsp/30mL dried dill weed with 1 tsp/5mL sea salt, 1 tsp/5mL dehydrated garlic, 1 tsp/5mL dehydrated onion, 2 tsp/10mL red pepper flakes.

Mack's kitchen hint: If there is seasoning left over, you can use it to flavor other dishes like grilled salmon!

™ Silhouette®

SPECIAL EDITION

FROM *NEW YORK TIMES* AND *USA TODAY*
BESTSELLING AUTHOR

KATHLEEN
EAGLE

ONE COWBOY,
One Christmas

When bull rider Zach Beaudry appeared
out of thin air on Ann Drexler's ranch,
she thought she was seeing a ghost of
Christmas past. And though Zach had
no memory of their night of passion years
ago, they were about to share a future
he would never forget.

Available December 2009
wherever books are sold.

HARLEQUIN
Ambassadors

Want to share your passion for reading Harlequin® Books?

Become a Harlequin Ambassador!

Harlequin Ambassadors are a group of passionate and well-connected readers who are willing to share their joy of reading Harlequin® books with family and friends.

You'll be sent all the tools you need to spark great conversation, including free books!

All we ask is that you share the romance with your friends and family!

You'll also be invited to have a say in new book ideas and exchange opinions with women just like you!

To see if you qualify* to be a Harlequin Ambassador, please visit www.HarlequinAmbassadors.com.

*Please note that not everyone who applies to be a Harlequin Ambassador will qualify. For more information please visit www.HarlequinAmbassadors.com.

Thank you for your participation.

BAP09BPA

HARLEQUIN *Romance*.

Coming Next Month

Available December 8, 2009

Whether you want to surround yourself with baubles and bells
or dream of escaping to a warmer climate,
you can with Harlequin® Romance this Christmas.

#4135 AUSTRALIAN BACHELORS, SASSY BRIDES
Margaret Way and Jennie Adams
Two billionaire businessmen, used to calling the shots, are about to
meet their match in the burning heart of Australia. Watch the sparks fly
in these two stories in one exciting volume.

#4136 HER DESERT DREAM Liz Fielding
Trading Places
After trading places with Lady Rose, look-alike Lydia is leaving her job
at the local supermarket behind and jetting off to Sheikh Kalil's desert
kingdom!

#4137 SNOWBOUND BRIDE-TO-BE Cara Colter
Innkeeper Emma is about to discover that the one thing not on her
Christmas list—a heart-stoppingly handsome man with a baby in tow—
is right on her doorstep!

#4138 AND THE BRIDE WORE RED Lucy Gordon
Escape Around the World
Olivia Daley believes the best cure for a broken heart is a radical
change of scenery. Exotic, vibrant China is far enough from rainy, gray
England to be just that!

#4139 THEIR CHRISTMAS FAMILY MIRACLE Caroline Anderson
Finding herself homeless for the holidays, single mom Amelia's
Christmas wish is granted when she's offered an empty picture-perfect
country house to stay in. Then owner Jake steps through the door...

#4140 CONFIDENTIAL: EXPECTING! Jackie Braun
Baby on Board
Journalist Mallory must expose the secrets of elusive radio talk-show
host Logan. As their relationship goes off the record, Mallory is stunned
to discover she's carrying her own little secret....